Faelorehn

Book One of the Otherworld Trilogy

Ellie,
There is magic
in this world if you
just know where
to look. 🌀

11·25·16

by

Jenna Elizabeth Johnson

Faelorehn

This book was written with Annalee Rejhon in mind.
Thank you for instilling in me a love for all things Celtic.

Contents

Faelorehn

One

Memories

he only reason I knew that I was awake was because of the pale green glow of neon stars staring back at me from my ceiling. I lay in my bed for a few moments, taking deep, steadying breaths while letting my eyes adjust to the darkness of my room. The remnants of a dream still danced in my mind, but as the approaching dawn light chased away the dark, it tried to slip away. Unfortunately, this particular dream was familiar to me, and it would take a lot more than my return to the conscious world to eject it from my mind.

I turned my head on my pillow and blinked my eyes several times at my alarm clock. Groaning at the early hour, I rolled over onto my stomach and buried my head into the pillow. I guess the darkness had some claim on the subconscious world, because instead of dispelling the dream, my actions only made it come racing back.

Huffing in frustration, I kicked off the covers and leaned over the side of my bed, scrabbling around stray pairs of shoes and forgotten socks as I searched out my current journal. Years ago the therapist I had been seeing thought it would be a good idea to keep track of these strange recurring dreams. Anytime I dreamt of anything that reminded me of my past before entering the foster system, I was supposed to write it down. That and anything strange that I saw or heard while I was awake. I hate to say it, but the visions happened more often than I would like to admit.

Although my collection of diaries held other frivolous information alongside the crazy stuff, at least once a year, on the same date, the exact same dream was described in near perfect detail.

I dusted off the cover of my latest journal, grabbed a pen from my bedside table, clicked on the lamp and opened up a brand new page. The dream was starting to slip away once again, but it wasn't as if I wouldn't be able to remember the details. I had written about this exact dream so many times before I could probably recite it in front of a crowded gymnasium without glancing at the page it was written on. Not that I would ever have the gumption to speak in front of a crowd. Nevertheless, I began writing:

I had the dream again; the one that always comes to me this time of year. The fog wasn't as thick as usual in my dreamscape, but I could feel the grit and cold of the blacktop beneath my bare feet. I looked down. Of course I was naked, but at least I was a toddler in the dream.

I paused and thought about that. I had decided a long time ago that the dream was merely a subconscious illustration of the saga that was my beginning. According to my adoptive parents, I was found when I was two years old, wandering the dark streets of Los Angeles (on Halloween night of all times), completely nude and babbling some nonsense that no one could decipher. I know most toddlers babble nonsense, but according to the woman at the adoption agency, what I babbled was nothing like what normal human babies produced when trying to communicate with others. Oh well. Like the bizarre dream, I can't explain that either. I was lucky, they told my parents, because the part of L.A. they found me in was notorious for gang wars.

Somehow, I survived that nocturnal stroll only to be reminded of that night exactly fifteen times, once a year for every year since I was found. And after fifteen years, I still don't understand why this dream won't leave me alone. I sighed and got back to my writing.

The dreamscape shifted and I noticed that my right hand was pressed up against a warm, solid shape, my fingers clinging to a wad of something rough and coarse. I could just see what it was out of the corner of my eye: a huge white dog, its bedraggled fur acting as an anchor for my small hand. The dog was massive, even from my child's perspective. I wanted to turn and get a better look at it but something kept my eyes trained forward, as if some crazy hypnotist was twirling a black and white spiral wheel in front of me.

The city lamps glowed an eerie orange, the only color in this black and gray world, and I leaned closer to the dog next to me. It padded quietly along, not making a sound; almost guiding me to some distant point of interest. I wondered what it all meant, but before I could make anything of it, I woke up.

Just as I shut my journal and replaced my pen on the table, my alarm clock started screeching and I nearly had a heart attack. I had forgotten to shut it off when the dream woke me. I tossed the sheets back and hit the snooze button, not even bothering to turn off my lamp. I wished I could sleep in all day but if I remembered correctly it was Monday. I groaned. Mondays were the worst.

After fifteen minutes of snoozing, I finally got up and made an effort to get ready for the day. I ran my hands through my hair and cringed. It was a tangled mess, but that was normal. I flipped on my bedroom light and stepped in front of the mirror glued to my bathroom door. Ugh. Sometimes I hated my wavy hair. Not straight enough to be considered elegant and not curly enough to be truly beautiful. Tully was always telling me how much she wished her hair had some curl to it. She has the type of hair that is so straight that hair spray won't even keep it in place after she takes a curling iron to it. She has no idea how lucky she is.

Taking a brush to the tangled mess did nothing but make it worse. Sighing, I made my way to the bathroom to brush my teeth and wash my face. For the only girl in a family consisting of five boys, I lucked out and got my own room and bathroom. Of course, the only reason was because my brothers were afraid of this particular part of the house, a converted basement that had served as a storage room to the previous owners. I think they somehow convinced themselves it was haunted, but that was only because it felt like the room was underground. It wasn't completely sunken into the ground though; more like the foundation of the house was pressed into the side of a small hill. The one wall facing the backyard had a sliding glass door that displayed a forest of eucalyptus trees disappearing down into the small marsh that sat behind our neighborhood.

I threw my brush back into the drawer with all the hair bands and hair clips I'd collected over the years. Staring into the mirror, I tried in vain to wish away all my flaws. Unfortunately, no matter how thoroughly I washed my face, I couldn't seem to make the freckles disappear. At least I didn't have as many as Tully. Of course, mine were darker. I scrunched up my nose but that didn't help either. Besides, I couldn't go around looking like an angry rabbit all day and it only made my nose look smaller than it already was.

Eventually, I caught my own gaze in the mirror and cringed slightly when my eyes stared back at me. I sometimes tried to convince myself that it was my awkward height and scattering of freckles that made people turn away from me, but I knew deep down that it was my eyes. They were the windows to the soul, so the saying went. If that was the case then there must be something dreadfully wrong with my soul if people couldn't even bring themselves to look me in the eye. I had trouble doing so myself.

On normal days my eyes were a light hazel color, too large for my face and slanted a little. People used to fuss over me when I was a little girl.

"Oh! What a darling little fairy, with that hair and those eyes!" they would say.

Memories

Then they would actually take a good look at my eyes and something would cross their face. A shadow or some subconscious instinct telling them something wasn't quite right about me. They would continue smiling, of course, but I knew, even when I was too young to really understand, I knew they had withdrawn from me.

I crossed my arms and let out a huff of breath. It was foggy out this morning and that meant my eyes would take on a grayer tinge. Yes, they tended to change color from time to time. Something else that made people uneasy. Sometimes I tried to tell myself that that was the real reason why people turned away, because of the color and not what they sensed lying deeper within.

After brushing my teeth, I slipped into my favorite jeans and t-shirt. My Monday clothes, because Monday mornings were just too stressful to have to worry about putting together a cute outfit. Even though I attended a private high school, it conveniently didn't have much of a dress code. Black Lake High, in the small rural city of Arroyo Grande, was actually quite laid back for a private school. In fact, our entire town was pretty easy going on the whole, but that wasn't unusual in the Central Coast region of California where perfect weather was a year-round phenomenon. When my parents first moved here just after adopting me, the Five Cities area was still relatively small, but over time it grew into a bustling rural metropolis of sorts. Fortunately, there was still plenty of open space to spare. I don't think my family could have handled living in a big city with me and all my brothers.

I was in the middle of stuffing my books into my backpack when the door at the top of my spiral staircase swung open violently.

"Meghan, you up?" one of my brothers called from the stairs.

"Yeah Logan, be up in a minute," I called back.

I quickly added a little foundation to my face (I'm not much for overdoing it with makeup), turned to give my unmade bed an accusing glare, then shrugged my backpack onto my shoulder and began climbing the stairs. I hardly ever made my bed, unless I was expecting company. That's a joke. The only company I'm likely to have over is Tully or Robyn. Tully's been my best friend since I moved in with the Elams and became their one and only daughter. Before that I was juggled between foster homes in southern California for the first two years after I was found.

I have to admit I was a strange child, still am, but I didn't know how to hide my oddities when I was that young. People were disturbed by me. Thankfully, no one ever told me I was strange and I didn't realize it at the time. In retrospect, however, the delicate way they handled me or the small glances they would cast my way as they moved further away should have been dead giveaways. I never did anything outwardly dangerous or disturbing, like starting fires or pulling the heads off my dolls, but I unnerved almost everyone I met and it took me a long time to get used to people.

The Elams finally took me in and were the first people to look at me as if I wasn't an alien from some other planet. They were patient with my fits and claims of hearing voices in the trees or seeing monsters in my closet. After taking me to several specialists, they noticed my improvement. When I started spending time with Tully, I started talking about hearing voices again. They tried to separate us but that only resulted in more nightmares and visions of demons. After that, they let me see Tully again. Somewhere in the middle of it all it dawned upon me that perhaps I should keep my visions to myself. I never complained about strange voices speaking unknown languages, nor did I mention seeing odd creatures ever again. But they never quite went away; they were all well documented in the boxes of filled journals collecting dust under my bed.

"Me-ghan!" Logan called out once more. "You'll be late again and Tulip won't want to take you to school anymore!"

Furrowing my brow and pushing the dark thoughts from my past aside, I returned my focus to more normal, everyday problems. I tried to tell if my hair was staying put. I had wet it and combed it out while I was in the bathroom, but it hadn't dried yet. Like I mentioned earlier, my hair was often at war with me. I liked to keep it long and if I treated it just right, I could get it to curl fetchingly and not frizz. Right now, I was happy with the waves that would form after it dried.

I climbed my spiral stairs and pushed the trapdoor open. I loved that the door to my room was set in the floor and opened up into a corner of our living room. A railing of sorts surrounded it so that my brothers couldn't sit on top and keep me trapped beneath. That didn't mean they'd given up trying, though.

I padded into the kitchen, carrying my shoes in one hand and my socks in another. I yawned, inhaling the smell of bacon, eggs and toast.

"Morning," my mom said, tossing her head so she could look at me over her shoulder.

She kept her dark hair short and at the moment she had a dish towel draped over her shoulder. I grinned. I towered over my mother. I was only an inch or two away from six feet, and my mom was nearly a foot shorter than me. Where my features were exaggerated, hers were proportionate and well placed. It didn't take a rocket scientist to know that we weren't blood related.

My father sat at the table, reading the newspaper as my three year old twin brothers, Jack and Joey, sat in their high chairs, throwing scrambled eggs at each other.

"Peter, could you?" my mother said in exasperation, turning to gesture a spatula at the twins.

Folding the paper with a quick flick of his hands, my father sighed and began speaking to my younger brothers, who only giggled at his chastisement.

Logan was standing on the other side of the kitchen island, packing his own lunch. He was a picky eater, so he learned early on that having such high standards in this family was a curse. He fended for himself most of the time.

Faeborn

Bradley, who was two years younger than Logan and seven years older than the twins, looked most like my father with his sandy hair and blue eyes. At the moment he was tormenting Aiden, my fifth brother. I never let my brothers know I had a favorite among them, and in truth, I loved them all dearly. But Aiden held a special place in my heart. Maybe it was because, of all my brothers, he was the only one with dark hair like me. I know it was silly; after all, it's not like we shared the same genes for it or anything, but it made me feel more like part of the family I guess. Or maybe it was because my seven year old little brother was autistic. We were both set apart from everyone else in our own way.

I dropped my backpack near the front door and walked over to scoop Aiden up in my arms. With me holding him, Bradley would have to make a real effort to get to him and that would only draw Mom's attention. Scowling, Bradley made a face and skipped off to occupy his time elsewhere.

"Good morning Aiden," I said quietly.

He glanced up at me with his big blue-green eyes. My heart ached for him. He hardly ever spoke, but sometimes I could get him to talk to me. My brothers teased him for speaking gibberish, but I always understood what he meant to say. Sometimes you didn't need words in order to communicate with someone.

Setting Aiden down but keeping him close to me, I maneuvered my way around the kitchen and quickly packed a lunch. Somehow I managed to avoid Bradley and Logan as they played a game of keep away with a cinnamon roll before Dad diffused the situation by threatening to make them all stay home Friday night and watch some Halloween special on TV instead of going trick-or-treating.

Five minutes before seven, I was heading for the door, Aiden clinging to my leg the entire way. Mom rescued me and came to scoop him up, planting a kiss on my cheek before I escaped.

Memories

The autumn morning was cool and damp, a thick fog clinging to the treetops and making the world seem gray. I didn't mind. I liked the fog. Taking a lungful of air, I traipsed down the driveway and started walking up the street, hoping that perhaps this day would be different than all the rest.

Two

Vagrant

I slowly made my way down the street, knowing Tully would probably be outside waiting for me. By some stroke of fate, we both went to the same high school. Both our parents were of the mindset that the larger, public high school in town had too many gang problems and not enough resources for so many students, so they were more than willing to pay the extra money for our education. Mom taught at the public high school, so maybe she knew what she was talking about, but in my opinion they were merely paying for peace of mind. It didn't matter what high school you attended, there would always be someone there to make your experience borderline miserable.

I sighed and kicked a pinecone across the surface of the asphalt, watching it bounce off the curb and skitter into the middle of the road. I couldn't blame my mom for sending me to the private school, not really. After struggling through middle school and junior high, she knew that high school would be even worse for me. I didn't get bad grades; that wasn't it. Like I was saying before, I was odd, different from all the other kids and I always would be. I was tested for every childhood psychological disorder known to man, but I never quite fit the profile for any of them. I heard voices and I saw things, more often than the average child, and sometimes I would go into fits of shaking or screaming and I would get terrible headaches.

My parents tried everything: medication, therapy, a restricted diet. Nothing helped. In fact, they were so desperate that they nearly took me to see an exorcist. I had been eight at the time, and they had the whole appointment set up and everything. Before we went, however, someone suggested a child psychologist to my mother. She was located in Los Angeles, my city of origin, and something about her description must have convinced my parents because by now they had had their fair share of doctors.

I don't remember much about the woman, only that she had a kind smile and long blond hair. After a few visits with her the voices quieted. I no longer saw monsters under my bed and the headaches eventually went away. Yet I still hear voices whispering in the trees every now and again, whenever the wind picks up and their leaves and branches rustle together. But I learned after those sessions with Dr. Morgan that to carry on about my unique experiences often frightened those around me more than anything else. Now when I hear or see anything, I keep it to myself and this has worked for the past nine years.

The sharp caw of a crow jerked my thoughts from my past. I glanced up, only to find something that was way too large to be a crow watching me from a pine tree in a neighbor's yard. Maybe it was a raven but it almost seemed too big to even be a raven. But what else could it be? I shrugged and continued down the road.

Three houses later, I spotted the giant black bird again. Was it following me? I sped up, passing four more houses before I bothered to look over my shoulder. Yes, it was definitely following me. I swallowed and felt beads of sweat break out on my forehead. *Please don't let this be another delusion,* I begged. The raven hopped to the top of a dead eucalyptus tree, arched its neck, and let out a strange, low garbling sound. It sent shivers down my arms. It turned its head to eye me once, then flapped its wings and disappeared into the foggy woods.

Faeloren

"Meghan!"

The sound of Tully's voice nearly made me scream. I looked up and smiled once my heart rate returned to normal.

Tulip Rose Gordon was my best friend and had been since her family moved into the blue, two-storey house that stood on the corner of our long, winding street only a year after my own family joined the neighborhood.

I took a deep breath and hurried over to give her a hug, already forgetting about the weird bird.

"So, how was your weekend?"

She made a face, her freckles getting bunched into the creases her frown created. Like almost everybody I knew, Tully was shorter than me and not nearly as thin. Where I'm tall and lanky, she is short and compact.

"I spent all Saturday trying to get through just a few chapters of that boring book Mrs. Swanson assigned, only to realize I had been procrastinating all day. So yesterday I had to make up for it."

I laughed. Tully wasn't a big fan of the classics, but she was determined to keep her grades up.

"I didn't do much either," I admitted.

For a few minutes we were quiet, standing on Tully's driveway and waiting for our friend Thomas to pick us up. He lived in Nipomo, east of our neighborhood on the outskirts of Arroyo Grande but still on the Mesa, a great tall, flat-topped stretch of land that took up several square miles of our part of the Central Coast. Thomas's mother ran a daycare out of her home so Thomas could usually borrow the family minivan several times during the week.

Tully and I decided to play a round of rock, paper, scissors while we waited. Finally, after defeating my friend for the fifth time in a row, the gold van came rolling around the corner.

"Sorry I'm late!" Thomas called from the driver's side window.

"You're not late," Tully piped up.

Vagrant

We climbed in and buckled our seat belts. The Lagarsos were a very traditional Mexican Catholic family, so the van was decked out with the usual memorabilia: Rosary beads hanging from the rear-view mirror and a postcard featuring the Our Lady of Guadalupe tucked into the visor. Thomas quickly pushed the preset button on the stereo and the faint, upbeat sound of Mariachi music was replaced by the newest teen sensation's latest song.

Tully and I rolled our eyes at one another, but our grins were wide. Thomas loved pop music but he was forbidden to listen to it at home. We laughed as he started singing along, and then against our better judgment, we joined in.

It was a whopping three to five minute drive to school from Tully's house. We took the few side streets that meandered through the expansive, wooded neighborhoods that branched out from our own neighborhood, and then pulled out onto the highway with the rest of the early morning commuters.

Black Lake High was situated directly off the highway in the middle of the great eucalyptus forest that covered much of the Mesa. On the other side of the highway the trees continued until they met up with the miles of dunes and farmland that comprised most of Arroyo Grande and the surrounding towns. The open space was only interrupted by the occasional farmhouse and of course the railroad tracks that were just on the other side of Highway One. There were other neighborhoods spread throughout the trees on the eastern side of the tracks, but the people who lived out here were even more scattered than my own neighbors.

Thomas chose a parking spot and turned the key in the ignition, cutting off some voice enhanced teen diva in mid-chorus. I zipped my sweatshirt up tight and arranged my backpack comfortably on my shoulders. School had never been my favorite place to be. I liked learning; I just didn't like being around other high school kids. They didn't get me, and they weren't mature

- 13 -

enough yet to be polite about ignoring me. It was much more fun to point out my awkward height or make some comment about my unknown parentage. Luckily, I had my small group of friends who were just as odd as me. As long as we stuck together, I could bear it.

As we crossed the parking lot I spotted our two other friends, Robyn Dunbarre and Will Abukara. Robyn was decked out in her usual Goth attire: black cargo pants, a t-shirt featuring a pentagram and black eyeliner plied on thick enough to make her look like some heavy metal groupie. Will was a contradiction next to her, what with his neat outfit of khaki pants, polo shirt and thick glasses. He was a walking stereotype, and being half Japanese only added to his geek appeal. All he needed was a knit Argyle vest and an overbite. Luckily, he didn't have either.

"Hey, did you see the homeless guy this morning?" Robyn sauntered up to us, the neon pink stripe in her hair falling into her eyes. She brushed it back with a ring-encrusted hand.

"Is he back?" Thomas asked.

I looked past them to see the object of their discussion. A week or so ago, this tall old man just spontaneously showed up on the outskirts of our campus. He was dressed in an old army issued trench coat, tattered and stained from years of use. He had been shuffling around one of the trashcans just in front of the school's office building, muttering and grumbling to himself.

Everyone had stayed away from him, not sure what he was doing at a high school. Right away, some of our more obnoxious schoolmates had gifted him with a nickname. "Hobo Bob" had not resisted when the cops finally showed up, escorting him off campus and taking him to some unknown location. Two days later, he was back, this time perched on the weathered bench that stood on the sidewalk in front of the public bus stop.

The police were called again but by the time they arrived, he was gone. He had been making special appearances on and off ever since, never really coming onto campus but never moving on.

- 14 -

I had no idea what he could want at our school. Most of us ignored him and I never even saw him approach someone asking for money.

"See for yourself," Robyn said, answering Thomas's earlier question.

We all glanced towards the far corner of the parking lot. He had on his usual trench coat, the hood pulled up to cover his head. The few glimpses of his face I had managed to catch had shown the weathered features of an old man facing hardship. He seemed to be staring right at us now. The prickly chill that ran over my skin proved my suspicion. I usually only got that feeling when I thought I was hearing or seeing things again. I ignored it and instead listened to my friends' conversation.

"Do you think he's looking at us?" Will wondered aloud.

Robyn crossed her arms and snorted. "If he's some crazy schizo that's escaped from the Men's Colony, I'll just have to cast a spell on him."

We all laughed.

"Can you actually do that?" Thomas asked. Sometimes I thought his conservative upbringing made him a little more nervous than the rest of us.

Robyn released a sigh and examined her black fingernails. "I've done it before."

Everyone was silent for a moment, but I only grinned. Despite coming from a very old-fashioned family, Robyn had somehow discovered Wiccan and Irish mythology our freshman year in high school. She went from being the perfect little goody-two-shoes to taking up her black garb and celebrating the pagan festivals of the ancient Celts. She always dragged us along to her little ceremonies, Thomas being the only one uncomfortable enough to feign illness whenever a solstice or equinox was coming up. I didn't know how her family dealt with it, but I think they blamed it on something that happened in Robyn's past. Like me, she had been adopted, but in her case I think it had something to do with extended family taking her in. Either way, we were both somewhat insecure about our identities.

The sound of the bell screaming over the din of car engines and chatting teenagers reminded us that, unfortunately, we did have to attend class that day. As we walked down the hallways, seeking our first classes of the day, I cast one more glance over my shoulder to see if Hobo Bob was still watching us. I didn't know if Robyn had secretly cast her spell or not, but the homeless man was nowhere in sight.

Three
Voices

The next day started out well. Thomas picked us up again and the morning proved to be promising. I didn't space out in pre-calculus, American history was actually rather interesting, and just before lunch I had my art class. I loved art, but only because I think our teacher was very much into letting us express ourselves. For someone like me, expressing myself in a non-verbal way, through art for example, helped soothe my psyche.

It was during the lunch hour that things started to go downhill.

"Out of the way homo!"

Like a rabbit that's heard the screech of an eagle, I jumped out of the way before I even saw Adam Peders. He wasn't addressing me, of course, but I could very well be his next target. Besides, I knew exactly who he *had* been addressing, and that knowledge made me ill.

I glanced over at Thomas, who was standing in the middle of the lunch courtyard looking for me and our other friends. In my opinion, he looked very much like a tree about to topple over. Thomas was even taller than me and a bit on the heavy side, so he always stood out no matter where he was. And apparently he was walking a bit too slow for Adam.

Before

"I said move you stupid fag," Adam repeated, giving Thomas a shove.

It felt as if someone had dug their fingernails into my skin. I *hated* that word. And he had pushed Thomas.

Thomas was so stunned that it took him a while to recover before he could recede into the space between our lockers. Everyone who had been standing around him had stopped eating their lunches and talking to their friends. They all stared at Adam. He might have been the star track athlete and he may have looked like some offspring of the Greek gods, but he was a complete ass.

As he brushed by, Adam pounded his fist against the closest locker, forcing Thomas and a few others standing by to jump. I ground my teeth. I knew Thomas was gay. So did Tully, Robyn and Will, and probably the entire school as well. We never mentioned it or brought it up for a few reasons. First of all, Thomas would deny it, probably because he didn't realize it yet. Secondly, it would only give the popular crowd the evidence they needed to torment him even more. And finally, if Thomas ever went home and told his parents, he might just be kicked to the curb. Yes, talking about it would be suicide.

A few minutes passed before the lunchtime chatter picked up again and Adam Peders's insult was all but forgotten. I breathed a sigh of relief, glad it didn't escalate into anything else. But my anger lingered. I didn't care if Adam's dark brown hair was always perfect or that his pale green eyes exuded flawless self-confidence. I refused to be like Rachel Thompson or Sara Hobbes or any of the other hopeless girls who allowed Adam's good looks to cancel out his evil deeds. Besides, we had history, Adam and I. He was the first person at my high school to learn I was crazy.

In kindergarten, those many years ago, when I first came to live with the Elams, something happened that my therapists over the years couldn't make me forget. Not even Doctor Morgan. We were coming back from a fieldtrip, the pumpkin patch if I remember correctly. It was October and I remember because it had rained hard that week and we were all covered in mud. My teacher had been holding my hand, because I had told her I saw something frightening as we traipsed around the great orange gourds. Of course, I couldn't really describe it but she knew about my 'condition'; my parents had told her.

When we returned to school, the house directly across the street was having some small trees cut down. I wouldn't have noticed it at all, but I was still shaken up by whatever had freaked me out in the pumpkin patch and I guess you could say my senses were heightened. We were almost all off the bus when the shrill, soul-wrenching cries of someone in pain reached my ears. I remember freezing and trying to curl into a ball. It took a few more seconds to realize the screams came from across the street. Between the buzz of the chainsaw and the crack of falling branches, I could hear the trees crying out, sobbing in pain as they were slowly being murdered.

I was so upset that I wrenched my hand free of my teacher's, and sobbing, ran right across the street without stopping, screaming for the men to stop their chainsaws. I was nearly hit by a passing car. My teacher was in a panic, the entire school stopped to watch in horror, and the men with the chainsaws were so shocked at my claim that they were hurting the trees that they merely stood there, staring at me. Luckily they decided to take a break then, but I could still hear the whimpers of the two birches they had just taken down.

I remembered two things as my teacher cradled me against her chest while carrying me back to the schoolyard. First, knowing the echo of those distraught cries would haunt me forever, and second, seeing Adam Peders staring at me with the strangest look on his face. At the time, I didn't know what that look meant, but now that I'm older I have a little more perspective. It was disgust, and even a little bit of fear. Even at the age of five, Adam managed to find fault in others.

Faeloreþn

"Hey Meghan, coming to lunch with us?"

I jumped and turned to find Will staring at me, his glossy black hair a mess as usual and his dark eyes magnified by his glasses.

"Uh, yeah, just wanted to put some books away in my locker."

He shrugged and moved on. We all ate on the benches provided for us on the north end of campus. There was a nice lawn with several trees circling it just in front of the school, but that was reserved for the seniors. I sighed heavily as I located my locker, and then stuffed my books in. I looked forward to sitting amongst those trees next year. The memory of my recent recollection surfaced for a split-second, but I shoved it back down.

It didn't take me long to find my friends. We always sat at the same bench, the one furthest away from the popular kids. I took a place next to Thomas and placed a comforting hand on his back. He glanced over at me. I could tell he was still shaken up. I pulled my lips in and gave him a small nod. We all knew what it was like to be the object of ridicule, but it was never easy for any of us.

That afternoon, as school let out, I glanced out Thomas's van window and spotted Hobo Bob leaning against a large eucalyptus tree on the corner of campus. I blinked as we drove past, for I could have sworn that his unusually tall frame looked less bent than usual, but when I opened my eyes again he was stooped over, examining something on the ground.

I huffed out a breath and pushed it from my mind. What did it matter if the homeless guy had been standing up straighter? Maybe he had just been stretching his back. I turned my head and watched the other cars drift by in the opposite lane instead.

By two-thirty I was already in my room, pulling my homework out of my backpack. I switched on my stereo, flipping the knob over so that it would play the CD I had put in last night. I smiled when I heard the violins begin their lively dance. I enjoyed a wide variety of music but when I was working on anything important, the soundtrack I preferred was strictly instrumental.

Like any school afternoon, I was able to get a good forty-five minutes of peace before my brothers got home. Once Logan, Bradley and Aiden arrived any hope for decent early study time was over. If they got it in their minds to torment me, then I would have to wait until after dinner to finish. I was really hoping my parents would enroll them in some after school sports one of these days.

Not today, unfortunately. I heard them arrive with the subtlety of a truck hitting a building. I tried to ignore them, but soon my mom was calling me upstairs to help get dinner ready. I sighed and set my pencil down. I didn't feel like working on pre-calculus anyway. I turned my stereo off and climbed the stairs.

Dinner at the Elam house was quite the production, what with there being eight of us and three of those eight being picky eaters. Mom didn't put up with it, of course, but that didn't mean my brothers never tried to get out of eating broccoli or mushrooms. I couldn't blame them about the mushrooms though.

"Meg, could you peel the potatoes while I go get Jack and Joey?"

I nodded and took her place by the sink. The twins were just a block over at a home daycare center. My mom couldn't wait until they were old enough to go to preschool.

I scrubbed the potatoes and tried to block out Logan and Bradley arguing over whose turn it was to play whatever video game they were currently addicted to. They took this time with their video games very seriously and counted it as preciously as a pirate would count his gold. As soon as Mom got back from getting the twins, it would be time for homework.

I cleaned the potatoes, clouding up the water in the sink with dirt, and then fished the peeler out of a drawer. I looked down when I felt someone touching my leg. I smiled. Aiden was looking up at me with those blue eyes of his.

"Help?" he asked.

"Sure," I said, "do you know where the colander is? Big yellow bowl with lots of little holes shaped like lemons?"

He nodded and padded over to the other side of the kitchen, then pulled the drawer open with a little more force than necessary. After a few minutes of banging around, he returned with the colander, dragging it behind him the way a smaller child would tug along a teddy bear.

"Thanks buddy," I told him, placing a hand on his head.

He wrapped an arm around my leg and I just let him stay there. He found comfort in such displays of affection and I didn't mind knowing that at least one person on this earth wasn't afraid to be close to me.

Peeling potatoes was a tedious chore, so I distracted myself by glancing out the window above the sink every now and again. I could see the neighbor's house, a little higher up on the slope than ours. Behind their house, the hill tapered off into the trees that surrounded the swamp. It wasn't a real swamp, at least not like the kind you would see in Florida or in some bad horror movie. It was just a low spot in the land that remained wet and marshy throughout the year.

I turned my gaze onto those trees and a flash of movement caught my eye. I strained harder to see what it was. Something large and dark. It flickered in and out of view as it moved between the trees. After a while I could tell that it was some sort of bird. Finally, it landed on the branch of the nearest eucalyptus tree, then turned its head and looked right at me with dark red eyes. I was so surprised that I nicked my hand with the potato peeler. I said some sort of kid-friendly curse, and then looked down to find a stream of blood dripping along my finger and into the dirty water.

I quickly glanced up again, only to discover that the bird was still watching me. It was the raven, the same one I saw that

morning, it had to be. But I didn't remember it having red eyes . .
.

Meghan . . .
No way. I couldn't be hearing voices again.
Meghan, you must come . . . it's been too long, we've missed you . . .
I closed my eyes and gritted my teeth. My hands clenched the edge of the sink. *No, no, no!*
Meghan . . .
No!
Meghan!
"Meghan?"
"Mom!" I said, looking around the kitchen as if I had just woken up from a bad dream.
"Honey, are you okay?"
There was a look of concern in her eyes. She got the twins settled in their high chairs and walked over to me. Her eyes widened when she saw my bleeding hand.
"Did you do that with the potato peeler?"
I nodded, then looked down and grimaced. The cut was pretty bad.
"I'll get you a bandage. Logan! Bradley! Turn those games off and come finish the potatoes for your sister!"
The boys groaned, but obeyed. I rinsed my blood down the sink as they made their way over. Mom returned with a box of bandages and some hydrogen peroxide.
"How did this happen?" she asked.
I wasn't about to tell her about the bird or the voices. Instead I shrugged. "I was daydreaming I guess."
She shook her head and clucked her tongue. After getting patched up, I got demoted to setting the table.
"Be careful with the butter knives," she said seriously.
I rolled my eyes but was careful to take her advice.
Dad got home ten minutes before dinner was ready and we all sat down and tried to eat like a normal family, but my father

insisted on watching his favorite trivia game show and the twins proceeded to make a mess while Bradley and Logan argued over who was the better basketball player. Aiden and I remained relatively quiet while my mom shook her head in disapproval over all of it. And so, there it was, a typical evening in with the Elam family.

When the dishes were done, I escaped back to my room in the basement and tried to complete my homework in peace. The only problem was, now that I didn't have the distraction of my noisy family, I was thinking about the raven and the voices that whispered in my mind.

I shook my arms out as if they had fallen asleep and turned my classical music back on, setting the volume louder than before. Perhaps I could keep the voices at bay with a piano concerto. For some reason, I felt the need to stand in the middle of my room and stare at the sliding glass door, as if some invisible force was beckoning me to look outside. It was getting dark out, and all I could see was my tall, gangly reflection staring back at me. Fearing that the raven would return, I drew the blinds and plopped back down at my desk. I needed to focus and forget about the stupid bird.

It was ten o'clock by the time I finished my homework. I quickly brushed my teeth and washed my face, then made sure my alarm was set to wake me in the morning. I left my music on a loop, hoping that the soothing violins would not only lull me to sleep, but keep the disturbing events of the day at bay.

Four

Illusion

To my great relief, the next several days passed by with very little drama. Adam Peders and his gang only sneered at us twice more that week, the creepy homeless man seemed to have moved on, and best of all, I hadn't seen the raven or heard any strange voices whispering to me in the night. All in all, a great week. I was actually surprised I hadn't seen or heard anything odd after that eventful Monday, especially considering Friday was Halloween. Historically, my symptoms always got worse during the days leading up to my birthday, so I didn't know whether I should have been jumping for joy or terribly worried something awful was about to happen. To be safe, I walked around with my fingers crossed.

On Friday morning, I rose early and put on my costume. I loved that we were allowed to wear our costumes to school on Halloween. Tully and I had decided to be butterflies so I wore my black jeans, a black t-shirt and a pair of antennae that we had made ourselves. My wings were yellow and black striped like a swallowtail's while Tully's were orange and black like a monarch's.

"Me-ghan! Breakfast!" Logan bellowed from above.

I checked myself in the mirror one more time, then grabbed my backpack in one hand and my wings in another and headed upstairs. I took the stairs two at a time, reaching the door that led into our kitchen just as my brothers pulled it open. I stumbled onto the tiled floor, too stunned to take note of the Halloween decorations hanging from the ceiling or the jack-o'-lanterns grinning from the dining room table.

"Surprise!" everyone yelled.

I squealed in irritation as Logan and Bradley attacked me with orange and black silly string. Being twelve and ten year old boys, silly string was a staple in their collection of ammo. Picking the sticky mess from my hair, I scowled when I noticed the curls coming loose. So much for cooperative hair on my birthday.

"Logan, you totally set me up for that!"

My younger brother grinned and shrugged, his sandy blonde hair still messy from sleep.

I quickly forgave them because when I bothered to look around I noticed that everyone was up and that Mom had made me a special breakfast. Aiden ran up and gave me a hug and I returned the gesture.

"So, do you feel seventeen?" Dad asked me.

I shrugged. "I guess so."

Not only did I get French toast with raspberry syrup and whipped cream, but my parents insisted that I open my birthday presents as well. The boys had pooled together to get me a basket of my favorite candies, along with a birthday card they had made themselves. Mom and Dad got me the new jeans I had wanted for months and a few gift cards from my favorite stores.

I was grateful that Robyn was picking me up that morning, because I was running late with all of the fuss over my birthday.

"So, you are going to the dance tonight, right?" Mom asked nonchalantly as I packed my lunch.

I rolled my eyes. We had discussed this earlier that week. I really didn't want to go. I wasn't much of a dancer and it was really more for the preppy kids who thought high school was the apex of their lives. I really just wanted to hang out with my friends at someone's house and tell ghost stories or watch some slasher flick or something.

"Yeah Mom, but I'm not sure what we're doing afterwards."

"Just be careful honey," was all she said as she reached up and gave me a quick hug around the shoulders.

The sound of Robyn's beat-up compact car lurching to a stop at the foot of our driveway drew my attention away from my mom.

"Okay, see you guys later!" I called as I grabbed my stuff and headed out the door.

Tully was already in the front seat so I squeezed into the back. Like me, she didn't have her wings on yet. I glanced at Robyn. She didn't look much different than she normally did, only this time she wore a full black skirt and a black and silver bodice decorated with what looked like skulls. The lipstick she chose for today was a brilliant red color.

"What are you supposed to be, a gothic witch?"

Robyn snorted as she jammed the car in gear. "No, I'm the Morrigan."

I blinked. "The what?"

Robyn sighed. "Hello! The Celtic goddess of the dead?"

I arched a brow at Tully, who had turned around to look at me. She barely fought back a smile.

"Oh, duh. Of course," I answered with my own grin.

"So what's the plan for tonight?" Robyn asked, as if her sacred obsession with Celtic myth hadn't been scandalized by our ignorance.

I cringed. "My parents think I'm going to the dance."

To my great surprise, Robyn actually nodded. "We'll just go for an hour and watch the lemmings paw at each other, then we can ditch," she said with her usual indignant flare.

"What are we going to do afterwards then?" I wanted to know. "My mom thinks I'm going to be at the dance 'til ten."

Tully was good about checking in with her parents. It made me feel guilty. My own parents trusted me too easily. Of course, I never so much as faked being sick to stay home from school, but now that I was a teenager they ought to be a little more strict. Not that I would ever do anything too scandalous.

Robyn grinned. "Hello? All Hallows' Eve? We're going to go down into that swamp near your house and light a bonfire. Duh."

She glanced at me in the rearview mirror, the red glitter eye shadow she'd caked on reminding me a little of that raven.

I shivered and cast the demented bird from my thoughts and instead focused on what Robyn had just said. That's right; another pagan festival was upon us. I wondered if Will and Thomas would join us this time. During the last 'festival', Will had had an allergic reaction to Robyn's harvest cakes and Thomas had felt weird about the poem she'd recited.

"That sounds more interesting than the dance," I said, adding my two cents.

Sure Robyn's little 'pagan parties' were bizarre, but I couldn't say they weren't interesting. But first we had to endure the dance . . .

Ugh, I hated dances, at least at our high school. First of all, I couldn't dance, second of all, the music they always picked out was just noise to me, and last of all, I didn't need some freshman or sophomore boy pawing all over me and then bragging to his friends later about how he had hit it off with a junior. No thanks. I may be one of the outcasts, but that didn't make me immune to the truly desperate.

"I'm in too," Tully piped. "I'll just have to let my parents know."

Robyn laughed. "Now we just have to convince the boys."

During our lunch break later that day, we outlined our plans for the evening to Will and Thomas, including Robyn's idea of ending the night with a little Halloween fest down in the swamp.

"Sure, why not?" Will shrugged.

I returned to my lunch, not bothering to wait for Thomas' response. As far as I knew, his parents were comfortable with the idea of Halloween but not so much so with the origin of the traditions behind it. I knew he would come up with some excuse about taking his brothers and sister trick-or-treating. We all knew his family was uncomfortable with Robyn's beliefs and we didn't blame him. But he must have felt rude about turning down Robyn's invitations time and time again, because he always seemed to make such an effort to politely decline.

"Do we have to wear a special costume or something?"

I nearly choked on my yogurt. Both Tully and I looked at him with wide eyes. He merely shrugged off our reaction with a rather reserved look.

"What?" he said. "I'm tired of everyone pushing me around. I'm curious to see what Robyn is always going on about. I told my parents I was going to the dance and then to Will's afterward."

We were all slightly shocked. So much so that Robyn, instead of laughing out right and crowing on about her obsession with the ancient Celts, mumbled a submissive, "Well, your Halloween costume should be fine." She warily eyed his thrown-together zombie motif. "It's just a bonfire really, nothing too freaky."

For the first time in her life Robyn seemed humbled, but I kept staring at Thomas, waiting for him to fold under the pressure. But the determined look on his face never faltered. Deep down inside, I gave a little cheer. I was proud of him. Eventually I concluded that perhaps Adam's public insult the other day was the straw that finally broke the camel's back. Thomas was tired of being a doormat; to his peers and to his family. He was beginning to stand up to everyone and even though this was a small step that only we would witness, it was a giant leap for his self-confidence.

After I finished my lunch, I crumpled the paper sack into a ball and aimed for the closest recycling bin, and then I leaned back against the sycamore tree, glancing up into the few leaves that remained on its branches. We had bypassed the usual tables today, choosing to eat out on the field behind the school with the few other outcasts. Normally we could spend the lunch period in relative peace, but that wasn't always the case and today was no exception.

We were minding our own business on the far side of the track when Michaela West, dressed in her cheerleading outfit, left the lunch tables and came sauntering over. I ignored her at first, thinking she was just headed towards the garbage can to throw something away, but when she didn't veer to the left I started to worry.

Michaela was short and petite, with a perpetual scowl and fake eyebrows. She wore her auburn hair pulled back in a tight pony tail and had way too much makeup on. None of us were impressed with her costume. She just used Halloween as an excuse to hike up her skirt and add extra padding to her bra. Some pale foundation and two red dots drawn on her neck suggested she was trying to be some peppy version of a vampire's victim. She closed the last few feet between us and crossed her arms.

"What do you want?" Robyn asked with sarcasm.

"Just thought you girls would like to know about this list," she said, completely disregarding Thomas and Will.

She pulled out a piece of lined paper from a pocket and flipped it in front of us.

"It's been circulated around the entire school."

I gritted my teeth. I didn't want to know what was written on it. It could only be something demoralizing.

Unfortunately, Tully spoke before thinking it through. "What is it?"

"Oh, a list of the girls Adam and Josh would never date even if they underwent plastic surgery."

Robyn made a sound of outrage and Tully took a small step back. I merely glared at the awful girl.

"Oh, it gets better," Michaela piped, flicking her ponytail over her shoulder. "People voted on who would be most likely never to have a boyfriend, too." She paused and looked up at me, her eyes bright with malice. "Do you want to know who got the most votes?"

Before she could continue, Robyn pressed forward and told Michaela she could shove her list somewhere where the sun didn't shine and grabbed my arm to pull me away. I had no objections to this method of escape. Insults weren't my forte, which was surprising since I'd had them thrown at me for much of my life. Apparently I was the catch and release type; I never bothered to dwell too much on what was said to me. Now I wished I'd tucked some of them away to use in situations like this. Luckily, we had Robyn. She produced insults the way a rabbit produced offspring.

Michaela shouted something nasty at us but I didn't hear her. I was trying to forget about that note she held in her hands. I know it was stupid to be upset about it but I couldn't help it. I knew exactly who had been voted as the least likely ever to have a boyfriend, and I knew why. It was me, and the reason was because I was so very strange. No matter how hard I tried to blend in, some part of my weirdness always seemed to seep out.

"Forget them Meg!" Robyn hissed. "They are a bunch of girls with no self-esteem and no brain cells. What do they know?"

I nodded. Robyn was right, and today was Halloween. It was my seventeenth birthday and I wasn't going to let some stupid, fake cheerleader ruin it. We would go to the dance tonight just to make an appearance, then we would go off and have Robyn's bonfire. Yes, it meant I was that weird kid I didn't want to be, but at least I would be among friends.

After school, I turned down Robyn's offer of a ride home.

"Are you sure? You're not planning on taking out Michaela and her posse, are you?"

I snorted. "No, I just think a long walk would do me some good. I'm going to take the trail through the swamp."

Faeloreyn

It was the truth. I pretended not to care about Michaela and her stupid list, but deep down it hurt. I didn't want my friends to know about it though. They would only want to comfort me, and although I appreciated their concern, I wanted to shake the feeling off on my own.

The wind rustled through the tall eucalyptus trees and I was practically humming as I headed across the football field and track behind the school. I found the trail that cut through the trees and ended up on a back road that led into the swamp. From there it would be easy to find the horse path that ran behind my backyard.

It was a rather pretty afternoon, the sky clear blue and the sun warm. The weather usually stayed that way through late November. I drew in a deep breath, truly reveling in the smells of autumn. I couldn't tell you what it was about the fall that made me like it so much. Maybe it was the idea that the year was coming to an end and soon the cycle would start all over again. Maybe it was the smell of hay and the earthy colors that accompanied the harvest that appealed to me so much. Maybe it was because my birthday arrived on the cusp of fall. Whatever it was, I liked it.

After passing through the tall trees, I cut across a side trail that had been worn through the layers of leaf litter and stepped out onto a quiet street. I pulled my cell phone out of my backpack and popped in my headphones. I searched my music list, looking for something that would match my mood. I decided to go with some indie rock today. I twirled a strand of my dark hair with my index finger and kicked at acorns on the ground as I walked. My butterfly antennae bounced with the rhythm of the current song and the yellow in my wings caught the sun of the autumn afternoon, leaving splotches of color along the road.

It took me half an hour to come to the end of the road. I easily climbed over the barrier that stated motor vehicles weren't permitted any further and descended deeper into the small wilderness that rested behind my home. The thatch of willows up ahead told me that the water was near, but I wasn't too worried about mosquitoes or getting wet. I would be through quick enough and by this time of year any significant amount of standing water was all but gone.

It was while I was crossing the small bridge of land that stretched beneath the low canopy that I first noticed something strange. I had been so busy humming along to my music that I missed it at first. A flash of something dull green, then the jerking and swaying of the reeds and brush ahead of me forced me to stop and pull the headphones out of my ears. It was as if an army of gophers had suddenly decided to devour the shrubbery around me. I would've dismissed it as merely some small animals foraging for food, but there were just too many of them and now that I didn't have music blasting in my ears, I could hear them too.

My skin immediately began to crawl, the way it did when my mind started playing tricks on me. It almost sounded like laughter, maniacal laughter; like some demented puppet from a horror movie had been let loose in the swamp. I swallowed only to find my throat had gone dry. And then I saw one of them. The creature was small and warty like a toad, with beetle-black eyes and teeth that protruded from what I could only assume was a primitive mouth. Reddish, bedraggled hair fell from the top of its head and trailed down its back like a horse's mane. Another one pushed the first creature out of the way, this one a little more gray than green, its hair paler. If I were to name them, I'd say they were gnomes. But they couldn't be, because gnomes didn't exist and I wasn't living in some fairy tale. The past seventeen years of my life were proof to that.

I took a deep breath and started moving once more. It was really happening again. The voices, and now I was seeing things. I guess I hadn't kept my fingers crossed long enough. I wondered if I should tell my parents this time. But that meant more visits to the psychiatrist and more medication. I wasn't even sure if Dr. Morgan still had her practice.

Faeborn

A sudden squeal behind me made me jump. I shot a glance over my shoulder. From the thrashing of the reeds and splashing of water, I could tell some of the things had gotten into a fight. Then a few of them tumbled out onto the trail. Several more joined them a few moments later. They were all hideous, gray and green and brown with warts and those strange manes running down their backs. They were only a foot or so tall, but they had vicious looking claws at the ends of their fingers and toes, and they seemed to be strong for their size.

I guess I stood still for too long, because one turned and spotted me. It let out one of those shrill, fingernails-scraping-a-chalkboard cries and threw itself down the trail towards me. My heart leapt into my throat, but I turned and took off, running up the sandy trail that would take me home. I might have been tall and gangly, but thank goodness I was fast. I put some distance between us, my backpack thumping painfully against my spine, my delicate butterfly wings snagging against stray branches. I never looked back, just pushed harder despite the deep sand. And I had been worried about mosquitoes.

After a few minutes I finally made it to my house. I jumped off the trail and cut up the slope, pumping my legs hard to reach my backyard. I dug my hand into my backpack and fished out my house key. It seemed to take forever, but once I found it I jammed it into the keyhole of my sliding glass door and pulled the door open. As soon as I was in, I slammed it shut and locked it, leaning on my knees as I caught my breath. Eventually, I worked up the nerve to look out into our backyard, secretly wishing it didn't open out onto the woods surrounding the swamp.

There wasn't a single creature in sight. I was confused, for I had heard them right behind me, even to the point of stepping onto the flat expanse of my yard. A flood of relief washed over me then. As real as it all had seemed, I had been imagining them. Thank goodness.

Illusion

Standing up straight, I took my hair down and walked into my bathroom. I looked like a mess. My face was all sweaty and dirty from the extra effort of running the last five minutes home, and I felt grungy. I decided on an early shower, hoping that the hot water would not only wash the dirt and sweat away, but would also cleanse away the images of those strange creatures from my mind as well.

The dance wasn't until eight, so as soon as I was clean, I was going to take a nice long nap and try to resettle my mind. I just hoped that my dreams wouldn't reflect what I had just been through.

Five

Samhain

I didn't dream during my nap, something I was very grateful for. If I had dreamed, I'm sure it would have been full of toady little creatures with sharp claws and black eyes.

I woke up to some Halloween themed song playing on my radio alarm. *Appropriate,* I thought. I threw the covers back and dragged myself to my bathroom, casting a quick glance at my sliding glass door as I went. I breathed a sigh of relief. No little monsters staring at me from beyond the glass; no scratch marks running up and down the door.

After brushing my teeth and washing my face, I sought out my costume once again. This time, instead of black jeans and a t-shirt, I pulled out a black dress I had worn to a wedding once. It had spaghetti straps and the skirt started above my waistline and fell to just above my knees. It was a little more formal than my daytime attire and the color ensured that I could still be a butterfly for the dance. After applying more makeup than usual, I glanced up at the clock. I had an hour before the dance started, so I grabbed my bag with a change of comfortable clothes for our bonfire, then made my way upstairs to wait for Thomas. Since his parents were taking his siblings around their neighborhood in Nipomo to trick-or-treat, he got to use the van for the evening, and since it seated more than Robyn's car, he was to be our chauffeur to and from the dance.

I climbed my stairway only to step out into a living room alive with chaos. Apparently my brothers were taking their costumes a bit too seriously. Bradley, dressed as some grotesque species of alien, was chasing after Logan with a laser gun. Logan, who had the bright idea to be a cheeseburger this year, was trying, and failing, to get away. It was just too hard for him to be quick in such a bulky costume. Aiden, like me, had invented his own costume, a super hero of sorts complete with a green cape and a mask. His favorite color was green, and every year his costume had to include that color.

My mom was trying to get the twins settled. She was dressed as a witch. Real original, I know, but she claimed it was easiest, classic and matched her personality when at work. She and my father always dressed the twins to match. This year they were a pair of sock monkeys. I had to admit, they looked pretty good.

Dad wasn't dressed in a costume yet. He had just come home from his job at the local power plant, but if I knew my father, he had some surprise costume hidden away. He wouldn't dare reveal it until he was ready to take the boys out trick-or-treating.

"Oh, look at you Meg!" Mom cried out over the ruckus.

I shrugged and did a quick pirouette. I shouldn't have. That drew the attention of the alien, and soon I was the target of Bradley's wrath. Eventually, I managed to grab a quick bite to eat and get out the front door without being captured or mutilated. Suddenly remembering my strange ordeal from that afternoon, I peeked around the corner of our house towards the end of our street only a dozen feet away. No sign of creepy gnomes anywhere. I breathed a mental sigh of relief.

I walked to Tully's, my nerves frazzled the entire way. All throughout the neighborhood, parents were trailing after their costumed kids as they darted from door to door seeking candy. It was getting dark, but I could still see clearly enough to keep a check on the shrubs that lined the street. It wasn't the dark I was afraid of, but what might be hiding in it. *Meghan, it was just another figment of your imagination, remember? It wasn't real, so stop being so paranoid.* Oh if only I could believe what my conscience told me.

Thomas's van was waiting in the driveway when I arrived. He was wearing his zombie attire again, and Will had added some gel to his hair to get that sexy vampire look. I didn't have the heart to tell him that his glasses kind of cancelled out that effort. Tully had on a dress similar to mine, but the skirt and sleeves were longer. Robyn was already in the van, her dark Celtic goddess costume looking the same as it had at school earlier that day. Once we were all buckled up, Thomas popped in a Halloween mix CD and we all started singing like idiots. Robyn merely snorted and mumbled something about desecrating the Celtic New Year.

The school was abuzz with activity when we pulled into the parking lot. We piled out of the van and headed towards the gymnasium with everyone else. It was soon clear that some people had changed their minds about what to wear that night. Many of the costumes were far more disturbing than what I'd remembered from earlier that day, some just flat out lame. A few people had tried to be clever, dressing as a cereal box killer or their interpretation of an infomercial ad. I wasn't surprised to see most of the popular crowd wearing something I wouldn't wear in my backyard to get a tan.

Robyn snorted in their direction and said with no small amount of sarcasm, "Because freezing to death in a skimpy costume is *so* attractive."

I nodded my agreement, my butterfly antennae bobbing with the movement.

The dance, just as I had thought, proved horrid. The music was too loud, the strobe light gave me a headache and if we weren't being ignored, we were being approached by the freshmen boys who hadn't yet learned that associating with us would ruin their reputations forever. We didn't even stay an hour. We quickly changed in the locker rooms and ended up leaving thirty minutes after we walked through the doors, sneaking past the teachers who tried to keep us corralled like a bunch of sheep heading off for the slaughter. I had no desire to be slaughtered that night.

We all piled into Thomas's van and took one of the back roads into the swamp. Thomas parked on the side of the dark street and we walked down into a small clearing beyond the barrier I had jumped earlier that day. Had it only been that afternoon when I'd been chased down by imaginary gnomes? Didn't feel like it. For several minutes I felt edgy, as if I expected those little goblin things to make an appearance again. But then I reminded myself I had only imagined them . . .

A fire pit, most likely built by the first teenagers who lived in this area eons before, was already in place on the far end of the clearing. As we gathered firewood I kept my eyes and ears sharp for anything unusual. We got a small fire started, and then we all looked up at Robyn expectantly. After all, this was her idea and we all expected some ritualistic words to be spoken or something. Not that any of us took this seriously. We were all just really interested in hanging out.

"Um, so I brought some information with me so you guys know what we are doing. Meghan, can you read it?"

Robyn handed me a piece of paper with interlinking runes as a border. It looked like she had found it on some website and had merely printed it out. I shrugged, curious as to why she just didn't read it herself, but took the paper anyway. I had to squint in order to read the words in the dim firelight.

Furrowing my brow, I cleared my throat and began: "Samhain: The Celtic New Year."

Well, that explained Robyn's grumbling on the way to the dance.

"It's pronounced *sow-when*," Robyn interjected.

Faelorehn

I gave her a harsh look that I hoped said, *then why don't you read it?* I bit my lip and looked back down at the paper. Sow-when; really? I shrugged. If Robyn said so . . .

"*Samhain:* The Celtic New Year." I made sure to pronounce it properly that time.

I read the entire first paragraph, which detailed the traditions and history of the Celtic New Year. According to Robyn's print-out, the ancient Celts claimed that the dark half of the year started during the next few days and that the veil between the Otherworld and this world became more permeable to the creatures and spirits of a supernatural nature. It was actually quite interesting, to tell the truth, and it kind of reminded me of all the other mythologies I had learned about in school. Of course, the sentence about Otherworldly creatures lurking in our world sent a tingle of fear up my spine. That particular description was a little too familiar to me with regards to my tendency to see things.

Once I was finished reading my part, Robyn took her paper back and pulled out a book with a pentagram and some other strange symbols on the cover. I felt Thomas tense up next to me, so I placed a hand on his shoulder. Thankfully, Robyn had picked out a pretty mild passage, something along the lines of asking the Earth spirits to protect us from the evil ones this night. I sent up my own request that the rest of the week prove to be vision and voice free.

"One way to keep the evil spirits away is by carving gourds or pumpkins," Robyn said after finishing her Samhain blessing. "The Celts used to carve turnips."

"How do you carve a turnip?" Tully asked.

"With a really sharp knife I guess," Robyn shrugged.

"How do you even know all of this?" Will added.

Robyn lifted her shoulders again. "I saw something on TV once about it and decided to investigate. It's amazing what you can find while surfing the internet."

Samhain

"So," I murmured, "do you have any turnips for us to carve?"

We all laughed, but Robyn shook her head. I had never seen a turnip bigger than my palm, so even if Robyn had wanted to carve turnips, I didn't think we could have made much progress. But I would probably have been the first one to start carving. Call me superstitious, but I wouldn't mind having a miniature jack-o'-lantern guarding my door for the next week or so.

Instead, she pulled a box of graham crackers, a bag of marshmallows and several bars of chocolate out of her bag.

"I don't have turnips, but I do have goodies."

Once we all had our own marshmallow roasting on the end of a stick, we started pestering Robyn for more information about Wicca and her other bizarre interests. Even Thomas took part.

I had never really taken Robyn's rebellious side seriously. She had a flare for the dramatic, so sometimes I wondered if her Goth look and pagan obsession was just a cry for attention, but it turned out she had done her research. Or so it seemed. I didn't really have anything to compare it with.

We ate several s'mores and after an hour of watching the fire die down, we decided it was best to head home. None of us was completely comfortable sitting in the middle of the woods with no one else around. We stamped out the fire and started heading back up to the car.

We walked in silence, perhaps all of us listening for the wandering spirits of Samhain. I thought about my family, probably still out trick-or-treating, if I knew my brothers well enough. Mom had likely opted to stay home to hand out candy and catch up on grading. When you taught English Literature to high school students, you had a lot of monotonous essays to peruse through.

I was so lost in my thoughts that I didn't notice the rustling bushes until we came to the point where the dirt road met pavement. I froze and shushed my friends. They all turned and looked at me with raised eyebrows.

"What is it?" Will lisped through his fake vampire fangs.

I waved my arm at him and told him to be quiet. Several seconds passed and the bushes rustled again.

"Hear that?" I whispered harshly.

Everyone nodded. And then I heard something else. It was the same, strange grumbling I'd heard earlier that afternoon. I felt myself go pale and I looked at my friends. I wasn't imagining it this time. They had heard it too. Maybe I hadn't been seeing things after all.

"Let's get out of here!" Tully hissed.

We started to walk briskly up the slope, the van seeming miles away. The creature grumbled again and we all screamed and started to run. We made it to the van in record time, everyone piling in and not even worrying about seatbelts until Thomas had the car started and rolling back up the street.

"What do you think it was?" Thomas asked, his voice strained.

"The spirits of Samhain," Robyn said, a mystical certainty tainting her voice.

"Robyn! Seriously?" Tully gave her an exasperated look.

"I bet it was a raccoon. They make a weird noise when they get into fights," Will added.

When we all looked at him with raised eyebrows he shrugged. "What? They do."

As we came to the end of the road and pulled out onto the highway, I listened as my friends babbled on about what had disturbed our party. No one noticed I wasn't talking and no one perceived how unnerved I was. I had thought I'd imagined it, I was certain. But if all my friends had heard it too . . . ?

"I'm telling you," Robyn insisted stubbornly, her voice only slightly tinged with amusement, "it was the spirits of the dead from the Otherworld."

Samhain

Everyone just laughed and Tully even gave her a shove. I was the only one who didn't laugh, because I felt strangely compelled to agree with her.

Six

Encounter

T he next day was pretty laid back in the Elam household. All my brothers were recovering from their candy hangover from the night before and my parents were still in their pajamas at noon. I spent the morning cleaning my room and trying to get ahead on my homework. I hadn't had a party for my birthday the day before, but that night I was having Tully and Robyn over for a girls' night in.

My friends ended up staying late, during which time we gave each other pedicures and talked about which boys at our high school were the cutest. Too bad they never showed any interest towards us. Robyn surprised me when she fessed up to having a guy outside of our school.

"Seriously!" Tully said, smacking her with one of my pillows. "Why didn't you tell us?"

Robyn shrugged and grinned sheepishly, a look that did battle with her dark eyeliner and lip ring. "It didn't start out as anything serious."

"And now?" I pressed.

"We have a date tomorrow night."

The movie we had been watching became nothing but background noise as we prodded Robyn for more information. I was happy for her, I really was. But something deep down, perhaps something instinctual, prickled with envy. I wondered if I would ever find anybody to make me feel as giddy as Robyn sounded.

Eventually the movie ended and our night came to a close. Tully and Robyn were gone by midnight and I went straight to bed. I remembered falling instantly to sleep and waking up on the dirty streets of Los Angeles. Wonderful. That annoying dream of my past again. It was essentially the same as always, but something was different this time. I looked down at my feet. Yup, they were still bare, but for some reason the distance from my eyes to my toes seemed greater. I held my hands out in front of me. Not a child's hands, but a young woman's. That was odd; I was always a toddler in this dream. At least I had my pajamas on this time.

Suddenly, without warning, the scenery changed and I was standing in my back yard. The moon was nearly full so its silver light cast long reaching shadows as it splintered through the silent trees.

I heard the near quiet huff of an exhaled breath and I glanced up from my self-examination. A great white dog was standing on the edge of my backyard, his ears perked forward and his black eyes watching me. He was as still as the night but somehow I knew he was beckoning me. I moved towards him and he turned and descended down the steep slope that led into the swamp below.

I knew I should have stayed put, but it was only a dream and I had absolutely no control of myself. I followed him without a second thought.

The leaves and branches crunched beneath my feet as I tried to keep up with the specter-like dog. Thank goodness he was so huge or else I might have lost him. Had it been a moonless night, he'd be easy to spot, but his pale color nearly blended in with the white pools of light.

Faeloren

He led me further along a trail, one I was familiar with; the same one where I was chased by a pack of warty gnomes just the day before. We walked for five or ten minutes, my spirit dog always staying twenty feet ahead and never looking back. Finally, the slowly descending trail ended and the dog took a sudden left, cutting across the small land bridge that split the lowest part of the bog. I followed him, eyeing the willows and oaks forming a dark, leafy bower overhead.

I ended up on the other side of the marsh, very close to the place where my friends and I had had our Samhain gathering the night before. A tall mix of eucalyptus and oak trees spread off to my right and the other section of the swamp continued far into the distance. Just off the main trail I spotted the small clearing where we had gathered. In the center of the clearing sat the dog, right where our bonfire had been, waiting silently for me to approach. I moved forward, my hand outstretched. Even sitting down, his shoulders came up to my waist.

Just as I placed my hand on his scraggly head, I woke up.

I was standing, in my nightgown, in the middle of the swamp behind my house. At first I was confused. Was this another part of my dream? But the sharp itch of a mosquito taking advantage of my bare arm brought me to my senses. I slapped the insect away, but my confusion was quickly being replaced by panic. Did I really sleepwalk from my room down into the swamp? I must have, how else could I have gotten here, barefoot, without a jacket, and standing upright no less?

I pulled my arms close to fight the chill and quickly darted my eyes from side to side. *There is nobody here,* I told myself, *stay calm Meghan.* But it didn't help. I tried to tell myself that the moonlight was bright enough to light my way home, and that the only thing in the swamp that I should fear were the mosquitoes. Unfortunately, I had seen some weird things in this swamp during the last few days, and I had a feeling that it wouldn't be any better at night.

Encounter

I took a tentative step forward and felt the sharp bite of a stick. Chewing my lip and cursing silently, I tried another, gentler step.

A low growling sound in the bushes behind me caught my attention. I stiffened and felt my blood freeze. It didn't sound like any dog I'd ever heard and I knew that we occasionally got black bears in the swamp. I tried hard to put that thought out of my mind. Unfortunately, in order to do that my memory decided right then and there to conjure up the images of the gnomes again. Would I be able to see them in the moonlight if they started coming after me?

The growling intensified and the snapping of twigs and rustle of leaves told me that there was more than one of whatever it was I was hearing. I cursed for real this time, something I rarely did. I glanced over my shoulder, back into the thick brush that lined the far edge of the wetlands. That was when I completely lost it. I knew animal eyes tended to glow orange or green if they were caught by your headlights or a flashlight, but only when the light hit them. Within the dark bushes I spotted several pairs of eyes, glowing continuously in the strangest shade of violet I had ever seen. I blinked to clear my eyes, hoping it was a result of my delirium from sleepwalking and the strange silvery light of the moon. I was wrong, as usual. There really were violet eyes staring back at me, at least five pairs.

Swallowing hard, I took a careful step backwards, seeking the soft, sandy trail that I had unconsciously followed down into the swamp. If I could only get back onto that path at least my bare feet would have a fighting chance. The animals noticed my movement and decided to leave their hiding places. Oh, how I wished the moon wasn't so bright.

The first one pushed its way past the undergrowth and stepped into the clearing. I tried desperately to convince myself I was still dreaming. I had to be; there was no way that what I was seeing was real. A monstrous beast, black in color and about the same size as the white dog I had followed here, stood crouched before me. The smell coming off it made my stomach turn, and that putrid odor mixed with the nervous fear that held tight to me made me nearly sick. It was horrible, as if the corpse of some giant wolf had decided to rise from the dead. From what I could see in the moonlight, great pieces of fur were missing and its muzzle looked almost skeletal. I would have given anything to have those little warty goblins back instead of these things.

The corpse dog snarled and released a long, mournful bay, a sound that made my already icy skin prickle with goose bumps. Two more monsters joined it from the brush, then two more after that. I was far too terrified to move and because of that they quickly had me surrounded, their violet eyes and rancid stench bringing me closer and closer to fainting. I fought it with all my might, knowing that if I did faint, these zombie wolves would most likely tear me to shreds.

I was trapped, terrified, praying that I was simply having a nightmare and that I would wake from it at any second. But the cold night air seeped into my skin and the gravel and twigs cut into my feet. The rotting stench of the corpse dogs assaulted me and the eerie silvery light of the moon only enhanced the hollows between their ribs; outlined the ridges of their spines. One of them opened its mouth and started panting, its throat glowing like a furnace, its breath pouring out in curls of black smoke.

I closed my eyes and wrapped my arms around my body, even though I knew I should have been running or fighting. I waited for them to launch themselves at me, wondering what was holding them back as they snarled and growled and glared at me, always moving in a slow circle.

A second passed, then another. But I kept my eyes shut, muttering nonsense to myself and waiting to feel the dull pain of their teeth.

The time dragged on and suddenly there was another fierce howl, more alive than the dismal baying of the death hounds. My eyes flew open of their own volition and there, fifty feet away, stood the great white hound from my childhood dream. He threw his head back and howled again, then charged the mass of demons surrounding me. The dogs turned and faced the new threat, snapping and growling and crying in that bone-deep, mournful way they'd done just minutes before.

I gasped as two of them leapt forward, biting into the white dog as he slammed into them with full force. The three that still stood around me were distracted for the moment, so I took advantage and turned to run away, only to trip over a fallen log I hadn't seen before. I hit the ground hard, losing my breath and destroying any chance of escaping.

The corpse dogs not fighting with the white hound lunged. I threw up my arm to protect my face, my heart racing faster than ever before, and screamed. A great yelp cut through the air, followed by a crashing sound. Then another yelp followed, and another. I lowered my arm and sat up, then nearly fell back down in shock.

Someone was there in that clearing with me. Someone tall and wearing what looked like a hooded trench coat. As I sat in the dirt, my mind and my heart racing with everything that had happened that night, I watched my rescuer, hardly believing he was there. Where had he come from? Wasn't he worried the dogs would attack him?

The monsters rose up from wherever they had been thrown, growling and looking angrier than before. I realized that the man in the trench coat had somehow knocked them back. How he had managed to do so, I couldn't say. The dogs had to weigh well over a hundred pounds and the man didn't have so much as a stick to fend them off with. Turns out, I didn't have to wait much longer to learn about his methods.

One of the dogs lunged, the speed in which it did so impossible for any living thing to accomplish. I shouted some unintelligible warning, but apparently it wasn't necessary. The man was ready for the attack, and just as quickly as the dog had moved, he swung his arms around and grabbed it, throwing it so hard against a nearby sapling that the tree broke in half.

I blinked and felt my jaw go slack. There was no way any of this was real. True, none of my visions or delusions had ever been this realistic, but this simply could not be happening in reality. A dream, like I had told myself before, it was just a dream and all I had to do was wait for it to wear itself out and I would wake up, safe and sound in my own bed.

My superhuman savior quickly took care of the remaining dogs as I sat and played air hockey with my own conscience. But before I knew it the demon dogs were gone and I was sitting alone in the middle of a clearing with a stranger who could move like a comic book hero.

The silence seemed strange, after all of the growling and yowling that had filled the air earlier. The moon shone down just as brightly as before and a slight breeze rustled through the willows growing on the edge of the swamp. I was too frightened and astounded to move, and I had no idea what to say. The man stood fifteen feet from me, gazing off into the woods that spread out beyond the clearing. He didn't make a sound. It wasn't until I heard the soft panting behind me that I realized I had forgotten about the white hound who had led me here to begin with.

I turned to look at him, standing above me, his tongue lolling out. I had never really gotten a good look at him before, in those dreams I had where he acted as a guardian of sorts to my very young self. He was solid white, except for his ears. I couldn't tell their exact color in the moonlight, but my guess was that they were light brown or even rusty colored. Or maybe that was blood from the fight. Of course, upon further inspection, I saw no other dark marks on him.

The dog huffed out a breath and then lay down next to me. I wanted to pet him, let him know I was thankful for his help, but some movement out of the corner of my eye distracted me.

Encounter

The man in the trench coat had pulled his eyes away from the trees and moved closer. I panicked, kicking at the ground in an attempt to scoot further away, but the dog kept me still, looking at me with curious eyes.

"Who-who are you?" I asked. My voice sounded weak and harsh.

The man didn't answer, but dropped into a sudden crouch, his elbows resting on his knees.

I squeaked and pulled away, afraid he might be one of the crazy people my mom had thought lived down here. What if he had a knife? What if he was a serial killer? All of a sudden, those zombie dogs didn't seem so frightening after all.

The man sat back on his feet, then hunched his shoulders over. His hood was still up and I couldn't see his face, but something in his stance was familiar.

"Hobo Bob?" I blurted.

I immediately cringed. I had never liked that nickname but that was the first inane thought that popped into my head, and honestly, I was a bit traumatized at the moment. I had just sleepwalked into the woods in the middle of the night only to be attacked by monsters. I think I was allowed a little slip of the brain for the next few hours. Or days.

"Sorry, I mean," I fumbled my words, worrying that I had offended the poor man. What was he doing here? Is this where he lived when he wasn't perched on the outskirts of the school campus? And furthermore, how on earth had he moved like that? The homeless man who had been hanging out around my school for the past few weeks was old and arthritic.

I was surprised when the man laughed. A light, easy sound that suggested youth. "Is that the title you have awarded me?"

I started in surprise. That wasn't the voice of a crazy old man. There was a strange accent to it, Irish or Scottish, and like his laughter, it was the voice of a much younger man. I tried to remember if I had ever heard Hobo Bob speak before, but I couldn't say for sure that I had.

And like the brilliant teenager that I was for the time being, my answer to him was a bland, "Huh?"

He laughed again, straightening up once more to his full height. I glanced up and gaped. He had to be close to six and a half feet tall, maybe taller.

"I often heard the spoken insults of the young people attending your school, but I never paid them much attention."

It was at that moment he decided to lower the hood of his coat. I felt my jaw drop again. Luckily, he was glancing off to the side, so he didn't notice my sudden gawking stupor. From what light the full moon provided, I could gather that my rescuer was a very good looking young man and all the names of the boys Tully, Robyn and I had listed off earlier that night seemed like ugly ducklings in comparison. His hair was dark and his face well-sculpted. I couldn't see the color of his eyes, but I could tell that they were dark, calculating even as he considered a stray stone on the ground beside his foot.

The light wind from earlier picked up once again and my body felt suddenly chilly. I looked down, only to discover that my night gown was hiked practically up to my waist, showing off my pink, polka-dot underwear. Flushing with embarrassment, I quickly pulled it down and wrapped my arms around my torso once again. I suddenly felt very vulnerable.

My movements caught the young man's attention and he glanced back at me. His sudden gaze made me blush even more. I hoped he couldn't see my red face in the moonlight.

"Forgive me," he said in a serious tone, "you must be very cold."

Before I could so much as blink, he had unbuttoned his trench coat and had thrown it over my shoulders, pulling it closed in front of me. His touch was light and careful, the opposite of what I had seen him do with those dogs. Despite the awkwardness of the situation, I tried to study him a bit more now that he was closer, but all I could make out in the moonlight was what he was wearing: jeans, a designer t-shirt, and what looked like utility boots, the kind my dad often wore to work, the ones with steel toes.

After draping his coat over me, he backed away. I caught a glimpse of something metallic around his neck, but it was only a glimpse. I had no idea what it might be. For a while, I simply breathed and enjoyed the warmth of his coat. It smelled strange, not in a bad way, but like something vaguely familiar that I hadn't smelled in years. I read somewhere once that scent was one of the strongest senses in recalling memory, but for now I couldn't place those memories. I only wrinkled my nose, thinking of these woods after a rainstorm.

At some point in time I managed to find my voice again. Clearing my throat, I said, "What were those things, those dogs?"

The young man grimaced and glanced off into the trees again. "Cúmorrig," he answered, "hounds of the Morrigan."

"What?" The Morrigan? Like the Celtic goddess Robyn had dressed as for Halloween?

He ignored my question. "Most modern day folklorists would call them hellhounds."

"Hellhounds?" I'd heard of those before. In one of my literature classes last year we had read some stories of mythology. I vaguely remembered a mention of hellhounds but I couldn't describe them. Guess I didn't really need to anymore.

I looked back up at the tall stranger, and feeling one of us needed to say something, I took a breath and said, "Thank you for helping me, and I am very grateful, but who exactly are you?"

He smiled, forcing the corners of his eyes to crinkle. I had to look away. Why couldn't the boys at school be this attractive? It might make their taunts more bearable.

"You were right in guessing who I was earlier," he said, standing up once again.

I had to crane my neck to keep an eye on his face. Even though he had the charm of a well-versed movie star, there was no way I was going to trust him. To wake up from a dream and find myself in the middle of the forest, surrounded by the living corpses of dogs, then to have him appear out of nowhere and chase them off with superhuman speed? Yeah, that was normal. Right.

He took a deep breath then ran both hands through his thick hair. I watched him carefully, not sure what his next move would be.

"Meghan, I'm afraid we've met under unsavory circumstances."

He glanced down at me with those dark eyes. "Our first meeting wasn't supposed to go this way. Those hounds," he paused and grimaced, "let's just say it was my job to take care of them earlier, and they slipped past me."

I blinked, feeling myself return to my previous stupor. What was he talking about? He knew about those horrible dogs? It was his job to take care of them? What did that mean? And most importantly, how did he know my name?

I felt ill, as if I were going to throw up. I tried to stand, letting the trench coat slip off of me. All of a sudden it felt like a net meant to trap me like a bird.

"Meghan," he said, reaching out.

But I cringed away from him, and offered him his coat with a shaky hand.

"Thank you again, but I really should get back home."

"Not on your own Meghan, not with those hounds still lurking around these trees somewhere."

His voice had deepened and that only made my stomach churn more.

"Please," I whispered, feeling the first prickle of tears at the corners of my eyes, "please, I just want to get home."

Encounter

Suddenly he stiffened and his gaze intensified. "You are afraid of me."

It was a statement, not a question. I knew I was doomed then. Wasn't it true that if a victim revealed to her attacker just how terrified she was, then she had already lost the game? Sure, he had chased off those dogs, but maybe only to keep me whole so he could take me off to some bomb shelter somewhere to torture me slowly. I shivered both from the return of the autumn cold and from the knowledge that I was completely at his mercy at this point.

The man merely sighed deeply and said, "I fouled this up completely, but I'll make it up to you somehow. Right now, however, I think it is best if you forget most of this."

He held up his right arm, palm out, as if he was planning to hit me with some kung fu move.

"What are you doing?" The panic in my voice matched the racing of my heart.

"Tomorrow, this will seem like a dream, but in a week's time I will send Fergus to you. Follow him, and I will introduce myself properly, at a more reasonable time of day. Then I'll explain everything."

I stared at his hand as he moved closer, wondering if I should try and fight him off if he reached for me. My mind seemed to grow fuzzy, my vision blurred.

Just before I passed out, I managed a barely audible, "Who are you?"

"You can call me Cade, but you won't remember this, so it doesn't matter."

And then I was swallowed by darkness.

Seven

Evidence

S unday morning brought with it a pounding headache and the
restless feeling of leaving a bad dream behind. I blinked
around my room as soon as I woke up. Everything was in its
place; my old TV with the crack in the corner of the screen, my
neon purple lava lamp, my posters featuring the paintings of
various artists and musicians I liked. And the old desk my mother
and I had found while browsing a local thrift shop, the top, as
usual, littered with the contents of my backpack.

The sun was streaming in through the sliding glass door,
reflecting off of the small droplets of dew sprinkled over the lawn.
For once it wasn't a foggy morning. Despite the normalcy of the
day, something didn't feel right, as if my mind were trying to recall
the dream I'd had last night. That wasn't unusual for me, but
something didn't add up in my mind.

I turned my head to the side, slowly so the headache
wouldn't escalate. A large blue and white speckled bowl holding
the remains of a few bags of popcorn sat on the floor, next to
several other dishes containing a variety of candy. Just the
leftovers of a typical night of overdosing on junk food and scary
movies. Nothing out of the ordinary really.

After struggling with the strange, uneasy feeling for several
more seconds, I gave up. It was pointless to try and remember a

dream that wished to stay hidden. It would come to me eventually, as all my dreams did.

I got myself ready for the day, flipping my radio on to the local classic rock station and slipping into my bathroom to brush my hair and wash my face.

I was halfway through my routine before I noticed the scrapes and cuts. I stopped and glanced at the scratches down my arms. In the mirror, my eyes peered back at me, looking more green than hazel just then. As usual, I wondered why. They weren't like a mood ring where each color corresponds with what mood you're in. Blue means relaxed, red means excited . . . Nope, mine just change color as my moods do, or even when I'm not aware my mood has changed. More likely than not, the change in color triggered my response.

I decided that my current mood was a mixture of curiosity and dread. How did I get those scrapes? I thought back to the week before, and then it dawned upon me. I had gotten into a confrontation with Michaela on the field behind school. On Halloween. On my birthday. She had wanted to show me a list. I had tried to get away from her. Only problem was, I hadn't noticed the chain that acted as a fence separating the track from the football field. I had walked right into it and fallen over, my books sprawling everywhere. I had obviously used my hands and arms to break my fall.

I rubbed the scrapes now, my face reddening from the memory. But there was something odd about it, as if it were a memory from several years ago and not a few days. An old memory.

Taking a deep breath, I tried to forget about the incident. I really hated Michaela and I made a special point not to hate anyone. But that mantra was kind of hard to stick to when you had people like Adam Peders, Josh Turner, Michaela West and all their shallow friends to deal with. They had been making my life a living hell since my first day at school when we were freshmen. And in Adam's case, even before then.

A noise grabbed my attention and I turned to find Aiden standing in the doorway of my bathroom, gazing up at me with those bright blue eyes of his. He startled me but I relaxed when I realized it was him. My brothers were always trying to break into my room, but they were always too noisy to be successful. Aiden was the only one I never heard climb down the stairs.

"Aiden? What are you doing down here?"

"Cartoo," was all he said.

I smiled. The medication for his autism seemed to be helping, but he still had a hard time communicating. For some reason, he had fixated on me as the most important person in his life and there was no way I was going to let him down.

"Alright buddy, is no one awake upstairs?"

He didn't answer. Sometimes he'd go a whole day without saying anything to us. I was used to it though. I carried him back upstairs and plopped him down onto the great stuffed couch in our living room and fished the remote out from between the cushions. I tried to convince myself that the sticky residue gluing my fingers together wasn't something the twins might have dropped in there the week before.

I surfed around until I found the station playing Aiden's favorite cartoon. His eyes lit up and he was hooked. When I thought it was safe to return to my room, I dropped a kiss on the top of his head and crossed back to the spiral staircase leading downstairs, passing Logan and Bradley on the way.

"Don't change the channel. Aiden wants to watch cartoons," I called over my shoulder to them.

They zipped past me, still dressed in their pajamas, their blond hair tousled and their eyes still droopy.

"What else is new?" Logan piped.

Luckily, his tone was cheerful and not spiteful. It was hard having Aiden in our family, especially since everyone else was so normal. Well, everyone but me of course. I think my brothers were pretty well adjusted, though. I glanced once more over the kitchen counter to find Logan and Bradley on either side of Aiden, all three of them singing the theme song to the cartoon at the top of their lungs.

I smiled widely, knowing that it wouldn't be long until my parents and the twins were up.

I descended my staircase to the sound of an electric guitar solo blaring from my stereo. I glanced at the clock. Just after eight. Why had I woken up so early on a Sunday morning? Oh yeah, the unremarkable dream that wouldn't leave me alone.

Sighing, I found a pair of semi-clean jeans among the pile of clothes on my floor. I grabbed an old t-shirt from my drawer and pulled that over my head. I promised Tully last week that I would help her with her English paper, but only if she would help me with science. We had a system, Tully and I. She helped me with my trouble subjects and I helped her. You see, I was a dreamer, head in the clouds, big imagination. I had an 'analyze poetry' type of personality. Tully was very scientifically minded; thought mostly in black and white. Of course, we both appreciated each other's talents, but I probably couldn't tell the difference between a DNA sequence and the number of chromosomes I had if my life depended on it.

By the time I made it back upstairs with my backpack and my books, the rest of my family had joined the fray on the couch.

"Where are you going so early?" Mom asked, a towel thrown over her shoulder as she mixed pancake batter in a bowl.

"Tully's," I said, grabbing an apple and a muffin. "Science test on Tuesday and English paper due Thursday."

My mom merely raised her eyebrows and nodded. She knew our system as well.

"Hey Dad," I said as I walked past his favorite recliner. How he could read his magazine while the boys watched unrealistic cartoon characters bash each other to bits was beyond me.

"Mornin' Meggy," he answered, his eyes never leaving the story he was reading.

I glanced at the article on my way to the front door. It was an exclusive on Stonehenge. My dad had a penchant for scientific and archaeological magazines.

"Well, see you around lunch time I guess," I said as I pulled the door open.

As the front door snapped closed, shutting off the sound of arguing boys and the clang of Mom moving dishes around in the kitchen, I threw my head back and took in a deep breath. The sickle-shaped, silvery leaves of the eucalyptus trees rustled in the breeze. For a minute, I thought I heard voices again: *dreams, full moon, memory* . . . they seemed to whisper.

I shivered, despite the warm autumn morning. That was the thing about the Central Coast; our best weather was in the fall. Sure, we had our fair share of foggy mornings, but on many occasions I had even walked on the beach in shorts and a tank top as late in the season as Christmas Day.

A heftier gust of wind pushed through the branches above my head, parting them like a curtain, and just as quickly as I thought I'd heard them, the voices were gone. Shaking off the weird chill and pushing the voices to the back of my mind, I hiked my backpack further up my shoulder and made my way down the road. I passed our neighbors' houses, their sprawling front lawns either enjoying a shower of morning sprinklers or lazing in the shadow of the tall shade trees. I loved our street.

I rounded the final curve in the road and headed towards the blue, tidy two-storey house on the corner. Bypassing the front door, I stepped right out onto the front lawn, shading my eyes against the sun as I glanced up at Tully's window. I smiled to myself, and then took out the tennis ball I kept in my backpack for just this purpose. I wound back my arm, took aim, and launched the neon green ball right through her open window. Less than a minute later, the tennis ball came whizzing back at me. I caught it and stowed it back in my backpack just as Tully poked her blond head through the window.

"I'll let you in through the back," she said as loudly as she dared, "Mom and Dad are still in bed and they want to sleep in."

Both her parents were professors at the local college. On Saturday nights they often ventured into San Luis Obispo to have a night on the town. Tully had once said that they were in denial about growing old. Of course, the fact that they had to sleep in until noon the next day did more to point out their advanced age than going to bars did to enhance their formative years.

Once Tully unlocked the door and led me upstairs, we started pulling out our books and notes. We chatted a little bit about the latest school gossip, but neither of us decided anything was all that new or important. Besides, we weren't privy to the good gossip anyway. Yet it still baffled me that for a high school consisting of just under six hundred students, we sure had a lot of drama that took place.

Sighing, I grabbed my notes on the latest English tragedy novella we were reading in our literature class and made myself comfortable as Tully grabbed her desk chair and moved it closer to me.

Only after I sat down on Tully's bed did it occur to me just how tired I was. I tended to be an early riser, so it wasn't like my schedule was any different than usual. But today I felt as if I'd joined Mr. and Mrs. Gordon on their club fest last night.

"Meg, what happened to your arms?" Tully asked, grabbing my hands and pulling my arms out to examine them.

"Oh," I said as I blinked away my sudden weariness, "the thing that happened with Michaela the other day, remember? When I tripped over the guard chain?"

Tully gave me a look. I knew that look. It was the same look I always got from other adults right before my parents decided it was time to take me to a new psychiatrist.

"You didn't trip over anything."

Faeforehn

"Yes, I did, you were there, remember?" Why did I always have to be the crazy one? "She wanted to show me the list of girls Adam Peders would never date in a million years? She hinted that you were on the list as well, or don't you remember that either?"

I was suddenly angry for some reason and it wasn't even at the insult the list had caused. I was angry because I suspected Tully was right. The argument had been real, I know that for a fact, but something about tripping over the chain wasn't quite right. Yes, it surfaced along with the memory of Michaela's pinched face but it seemed misplaced, contrived even. Like when you were a toddler and you were trying to figure out how to piece together a jigsaw puzzle for the first time in your life. Although the pieces don't quite fit, you tried to force them together anyway.

Tully glanced up at me with her clear green eyes. I normally towered over her, but at that moment she made me feel as small as my twin brothers.

"I remember you tripping over a chain fence," she whispered, "but that was in third grade when Marissa Campos told us she knew how to make our freckles multiply."

Both of us released a laugh at the memory, and the tension that had been building up melted a little bit.

"I, I'm sorry Tully," I whispered, hiding my arms and the scratches covering them from her view. "Do you promise not to freak out if I tell you the truth?"

Tully raised her right hand and crossed her heart with her index finger.

"I don't know how I got these scrapes." I held my arms out in front of me again, as if looking at them would give me the answer.

"How can you not remember?" Tully insisted. "They look pretty new. Are there any others, I mean, not just on your arms?"

"Yeah, my knees actually, and I feel like I'm going to be finding bruises all over the place in a day or two."

Evidence

"Did you fall down yesterday, maybe playing basketball with your brothers?" Tully asked.

I actually considered it, and to tell the truth, I couldn't remember much of what *had* happened yesterday, not much at all. When I told Tully this she furrowed her brow and sighed. "It's like someone has erased your memory."

As if Tully's words were the snap of a hypnotist's fingers, part of my dream from the night before surfaced in my mind. An image of a white dog and trees standing stark against the light of the near-full moon flashed across my vision. Unfortunately, it was gone before I could get a good hold of it.

I sighed again.

"Maybe you hit your head when you got hurt, and are suffering from amnesia."

I shrugged, then suggested we drop the subject altogether and focus on our homework. Tully readily agreed with me. I think deep down we were both a little rattled by the whole thing, and right then and there I had no answers to offer.

When I got home later that day, I decided I needed a nap. Mom thought I might be getting sick, but I just waved her off and said that studying for science often made me brain dead for an hour or two anyway. As I crossed the living room I saw Dad's magazine sitting askew atop the coffee table. A familiar image of Stonehenge dominated the cover and for some strange reason I recalled noticing that before, when I had left that morning.

A terrifying image shot through my mind then, of a dark forest scene crowded with the rotting corpses of dogs, a moonlit meadow and something else I couldn't quite see . . . I gasped, the burning image of glowing, violet eyes piercing my skull.

My mom was at my side before I completely lost my composure.

"Meghan! Meghan, what's wrong?"

"I'm okay Mom," I mumbled as I clutched my head. It didn't really hurt, my head, but the sudden return of details from what must have been my dream from the night before had shocked me that much.

"What's the matter?" she pressed, using her petit frame to keep me on my feet.

I thought lying was the best choice in this situation. "Headache," I grumbled.

I had had migraines when I was younger, in the years after they found me in Los Angeles, and a few since then, so it wasn't a complete impossibility. In order to add to the act, I pressed my arm against my forehead. Too bad I had forgotten about the scrapes.

"Meghan! What did you do to your arms?"

"Uhh," I answered dully, "tripped in P.E. on Thursday. We were playing softball."

The grumbling sound next to my ear told me that she chose to believe my story, for the time being at least. She helped me down the spiral staircase that descended into my room.

"You'll kill yourself climbing down if I don't help you," she insisted.

Once downstairs, I sat on the edge of my bed and told her I could take it from there. She stayed for a bit longer, closing the blinds that hung from my sliding glass door while making comments under her breath about my messy room and its likely contribution to my headache. Mom liked things immaculate.

Finally she left, but only after I feigned lying down and going to sleep. I listened to her footfalls as she climbed the carpeted steps, but even after she had closed the door behind her, I stayed in bed, my forearm over my forehead and my eyes glued to the glowing stars stuck to the ceiling.

Only after my breathing evened out and I no longer felt the waves of terror flooding over me, did I allow my thoughts to wander back to my nightmare from the night before, and most likely, the reason for my current state of scraped skin and exhaustion.

Eight

Familiar

O f course, no answers ever came to me and after an hour of agonizing reflection, I came to the conclusion that I had simply had a nightmare the evening before and that my scrapes and bruises had been a result of a violent case of sleepwalking. Though my room remained fully intact, I knew there was no other explanation.

Despite the fact that there were still bits and pieces of my dream missing, I felt somewhat satisfied with my conclusion. After all, it wasn't like I had never forgotten a dream I'd had before.

I joined my family for dinner, putting on my freshest face and brushing aside any concerns they voiced aloud. Of course, my mother was the only one to display any true worry. The boys had no idea I had almost fainted (they had been at the grocery story with my dad when I had first come home from Tully's). Dad had merely given me his customary once over. As long as we had all our limbs and weren't hemorrhaging from the head, there was absolutely nothing wrong with us.

After dinner we huddled down to watch TV before Mom and Dad started getting the twins and Aiden ready for bed. They all complained when the time arrived, but somehow my parents managed. Logan and Bradley soon followed, grumbling about how late it wasn't and how they weren't even tired as they yawned and rubbed their eyes. I grinned, finding something amusing in their simple, childhood woes.

Yawning, I called a goodnight to my parents. I had school in the morning, hurrah, and a test early in the week. It would do me no good to start the week out cranky and tired. I clambered down my spiral staircase, half eager for the warmth of my bed, half afraid of what would happen once I fell asleep.

The visions and voices and nightmares were returning, I could deny it no longer, but I wasn't sure I could deal with it again. I couldn't go back into therapy and the medication I had taken when I was younger had made me feel nauseous all the time. And the truth of it was, it never really helped. I only pretended that it did so they wouldn't give me more of the awful medicine. Like before, I would just have to find a way to ignore my visions. If I was lucky, in a week or two everything would go back to normal once again. I pulled on my pajamas and curled into bed, counting imaginary pink and yellow butterflies visiting white flowers as I tried to keep my frightening memories at bay.

Monday morning was a riot in our house, as usual. I packed a lunch and grabbed my backpack, squeezing out the front door right before Jack and Joey started throwing cereal at one another. The morning was foggy once again, that nice thick fog that rolled in from the Pacific Ocean and nestled itself in the lower areas of the coast.

I strolled along the side of the road, making my way down to Tully's. A group of middle school kids waited for their bus on the corner of the street. Today they stood huddled around the street sign, the older kids trying to look cool while the little kids picked up acorns and launched them at one another.

As I watched, something caught the corner of my eye. I turned and glimpsed the dark sweep of a bird's wing disappearing into the redwood that stood behind the wide stone barrier wall that denoted our neighborhood. I stared at the spot where the wing had disappeared, thinking it was just a crow. As I watched, however, the bird edged closer to a gap between the drooping branches.

I sucked in a breath. The thing was huge, nearly as big as an eagle, and it stared, no, *glared* right at me. Not for the first time that week, an icy chill prickled up my spine. *No freaking way.* It was the raven from last week. I knew it without a doubt. Unless, of course, there happened to be huge ravens lurking about our area lately, and I highly doubted that. I cast another wary glance at the bird. It appeared to be thinking, calculating, deciding whether or not it wished to eat my eyes or my liver first.

"Meghan!"

I nearly screamed. Instead, I jumped and let out a pitiful noise that sounded closer to a Chihuahua yelping. All the kids at the bus stop turned and looked at me. Most of them started to laugh and point.

Feeling my cheeks turn pink, I turned towards Tully, who also had a big grin on her face.

"Get out much in this wide world?" she teased.

I grumbled at her and marched to her driveway where her mom's car waited. She had the flu or something, so Tully was allowed to drive the car to school. Despite our advanced ages, we still didn't have our own cars. Vehicles were necessary in a rural town, but they were also expensive. I understood that. My parents weren't destitute by any means, but having all us kids took a toll on their finances. Luckily, I had friends to bum rides off of.

I threw my backpack into the back seat of the silver station wagon with Tully's and we climbed in. As we pulled up to the stop sign, I looked back up into the redwood tree. I told myself it was to avoid eye contact with the kids I had embarrassed myself in front of, but I really wanted to know if the raven was still there. To my great relief, or perhaps disappointment (I honestly couldn't say which), the unnerving bird was gone.

Faeloren

Just another hallucination, I told myself as the car chugged along, *just another figment of your imagination.*

When we pulled into the high school parking lot five minutes later, I found myself scanning the edge of our campus.

I had no idea I was doing it until Tully asked, "Whatcha looking for?"

"Nothing," I said automatically, leaning back into the seat and basking in the warmth of the car's heater for a bit longer. The day would warm up, once the fog wore off, but at the moment it was cold and damp.

I sighed and glanced back out the window. What *had* I been looking for? As we found a place to park, I reached into the back of the seat and grabbed my backpack. Through the rear window I could see the bench where the local public bus stopped. I froze, my hand clutching the strap of my backpack to the point where my knuckles turned white. It was then that I became aware of what I had been searching for. The homeless man was back, sitting hunched over on the bench as if he were asleep.

Why in the world had I wanted to find him? An image of a tall man dressed in a hooded trench coat flashed before my eyes. I felt my face drain of color and my palms go clammy.

"Hey Meghan, you don't look so good. You're not feeling sick are you?" Tully asked.

I swallowed, only to find my mouth had gone dry as well. "I'm fine," I managed, sounding somewhat normal.

Tully shrugged and smoothed out her skirt and pulled up her neon-striped leggings. Most people would call her sense of style flashy or a bad reproduction of the Eighties, but I couldn't imagine any other style that would reflect her personality so well.

"Hey girls, what's up?" Robyn called from across the parking lot.

The majority of the student body made way for her. Considering they all dressed and acted like they lived inside some high end fashion catalog, I was never surprised when they got out of Robyn's way. I grinned.

Just then, the bell rang, signaling the start of school. We all grimaced.

"Well, time to get another Monday underway!" Robyn proclaimed.

Unfortunately, I didn't share her enthusiasm.

I managed to survive the week without encountering too many misfortunes. My science test wasn't a complete disaster and the people in my geography group were the types who strove for good grades.

On Friday, Robyn gave Tully and I a ride home, so after my last class I gathered my books from my locker and headed out to the parking lot. We piled into her old car just before the lemmings poured out of the hallways. I always smirked when I thought of that nickname for the popular crowd and their followers. Robyn had thought of it, of course.

"They're like lemmings! They would all follow each other off of a cliff if that was the cool thing to do. Completely mindless," she had said in disgust. The name has stuck ever since.

They each had their own cars, every one of them much newer than any of my friends' vehicles of course, and often cut us off as we all made a mad dash for the exit. For some reason, however, they never bothered us when Robyn drove. I couldn't tell if it was her tendency to cut corners a little too close, or if the state of her car itself acted as a deterrent. I didn't care. As long as they stayed away I was happy.

As we pulled out of the parking lot and onto the tree-lined highway, I caught a glimpse of someone standing just within the tree line. It was Hobo Bob. My heart lurched and the hair stood up on my arms, though I couldn't say why. I couldn't figure out why he bothered me so much. He hadn't been hanging around as much as before, and it wasn't as if he ever approached any of us or shuffled around muttering and shouting random curse words. A thought flashed through my head, not as vivid as the one last Sunday of the weird dogs, but clearer. A picture of me standing in the clearing in the swamp where my friends and I had enjoyed the bonfire on Halloween. Only, it wasn't dark out and I was wearing jeans and an old t-shirt. Just as quickly, the thought flickered away. I shook my head. Oh well.

I made it home in time to learn that my mom had decided we were all going out together to see a movie. This was a rare occurrence, since going to an actual movie theater cost an arm and a leg these days. I went to my room to deposit my backpack and put on a warmer shirt. Even Dad was going this time, and he grumbled as he grabbed the keys to our SUV. Usually I was on Dad's side; we always had to go see a kid's movie because of Aiden and the twins, and I could usually argue on behalf of the both of us. But tonight I welcomed a distraction, even a ridiculous one.

The movie, of course, was terrible. The plot was shallow and the main character was a talking rodent who thought that noisy bodily functions were the height of comedy. Naturally, my brothers liked it and my mother laughed along with them. Dad had the luxury of falling asleep but I merely gritted my teeth and bore it.

By the time we got home it was dark and time for the boys to go to bed. I feigned exhaustion and headed downstairs as well. I settled in bed and picked up the remote to my old TV. After seeing tonight's movie, I needed something substantial to drag me back from what had been equivalent to cinema trash. Just my luck, an old classic adventure was on. The movie was already halfway over but it was more than enough to revive my spirits.

I fell asleep just as the main characters were fighting their way towards freedom. Perhaps that explains the dream I had. I was running through a forest somewhere, not the one behind my home, but one that seemed more primitive, with oaks and beech trees that had to be hundreds of years old. I kept tripping on their roots as I ran, my feet bare once again, the hem of my old sweat pants loose around my ankles as I struggled to stay ahead of something. At one point, I glanced down and screamed. It wasn't roots I was tripping over but long, skinny, stick-like arms and fingers that reached out from the brush, gripping at my ankles.

Finally, one managed a decent grasp and I fell forward, my hands skidding in mud and leaf litter. I rolled over, panting hard, my loose hair sticking to my sweaty face, and saw glowing eyes above me. These ones were red and the only other thing I could see in the dark was several pairs of long incisors, leaning down to devour me.

I woke with a start and, I'm pretty certain, a startled shout. I blinked around my room, taking deep breaths as my heart began to slow its erratic beating. I groaned and fell back onto my pillows. My sheets were soaked with sweat and my head was pounding. So much for ignoring my dreams and visions. I cracked open an eye and glanced out my sliding glass door. Just before dawn, if I was guessing right. Sighing, I flung my sheets back and marched into my bathroom. I was tired, but I hated the feeling of cold sweat, so I thought a shower would be a good idea.

The hot water and fragrant scent of my lavender soap woke me up. Once dry, I pulled on a pair of old jeans and wrapped a towel around my torso. I walked back out into my room and opened my dresser. Of course, there was only one clean t-shirt left. Guess it was time to do some laundry.

I pulled the shirt out. It was rusty orange and portrayed the emblem of some summer camp I had attended a year or two before. The color caught my attention more than anything. The vision of me standing in the swamp wearing jeans and a t-shirt came back. Yup, the t-shirt had been this exact color. My skin prickled from the strangeness again.

Doesn't mean anything, I told myself as I pulled the shirt over my wet head.

Faeloren

Along with hearing voices and having bad dreams, I had often times had premonitions as a child. When I was six, I burst into my parents' room, crying because I had seen Rugby get hit by a car. Rugby was our family cat. My parents cajoled me and told me Rugby was fine. I wasn't convinced. But he showed up that evening for his dinner and a few games of chase-the-string with my mom. At the end of the week, however, my dad found him on the side of the highway. We buried him in the backyard and planted an azalea over him. The azalea was now full grown, but we never got another cat after that.

That wasn't the only time. When I was twelve, I dreamt that Bradley would fall and break his arm when we were playing on the slope behind our house. It was something he had said in my dream that triggered it, and when he repeated the same words, I jumped in front of him before he could leap onto the log that was about to give way.

Little premonitions, really, but enough to make anyone else worry. For a while, I thought I might have a sixth sense, but then the premonitions went away. Now I was beginning to wonder if they were coming back, along with everything else.

I sighed and flipped on the hair dryer. Once fully dressed and my curly hair reasonably tamed, I returned to my room to make my bed. That's when I saw him, standing outside my sliding glass door. I froze and blinked, wondering if he was real.

He stood ten feet from the glass, just on the edge of the concrete patch that served as a small patio. He was as still as a statue and looked like white marble in the dim, early morning light. I was afraid to blink again, in case he disappeared.

A name floated up from my buried thoughts. "Fergus," I whispered, wondering where on earth that name had come from.

The great white hound opened his mouth and his tongue lolled happily as he panted. He turned and trotted away across my backyard, his loping gait easy and smooth.

Familiar

I cursed, half-mesmerized and half-panicked. Something was urging me to follow him, something I couldn't control. Something instinctual, something . . . primitive.

Without another thought, I grabbed my shoes and shoved them onto my feet. I snatched my sweatshirt off the back of my desk chair and taking one more glance at my desktop, decided to go prepared this time. Fishing into my backpack, I found the small container of pepper spray I always kept there and shoved it into my pocket.

As the sun was just cresting the eastern horizon, its rays piercing the morning fog, I made my way down the steep slope into the woods of the swamp, puffing against the cold air and wondering if it was a ghost I was chasing. Wondering if I really was crazy after all.

-Nine-
Revelation

I was halfway to the clearing when I remembered why I had avoided these woods for the past week. Last time I was walking this particular path, I had been moving in the opposite direction, trying desperately to escape a herd of demented garden gnomes. At least this time I had my pepper spray, though I wasn't so sure pepper spray would work against a hallucination.

Despite my wariness, I trudged on. The morning was cool, the fog slow to burn off. I pulled my sweatshirt on and tucked my hands under my armpits and listened for any unusual sounds. The only thing I could hear was the familiar drip-splat of the condensation falling from the leaves. Even the footfalls of the huge dog several yards in front of me were silent, eerily so. As I followed him, I wondered what had gotten into me of late. I never was the type to seek out adventure or go off on my own if I wasn't comfortable, or familiar, with the outcome. Any minute, those freakish gnomes could show up again. No, at any moment I could start seeing things again and if anyone happened to be hiking down here and saw me running in terror from nothing, well, let's just say my reputation didn't need any more damage.

I sighed, the smell of eucalyptus oil and the dampness that lingered around swamps flooding my senses. I shook my head and took note of how far we had traveled down the equestrian trail; about halfway between my house and the lowest point of the swamp.

The great hound vanished around a bend guarded by a small thicket of arroyo willows.

"Hey, dog, wait up!" I called after it. Another tally to add to the 'signs Meghan is crazy' chart.

Of course, the dog didn't wait up and by the time I made it to the bend in the path, he had disappeared. I grumbled and considered turning around and going home. This was ridiculous. What had enticed me out here in the first place? I would have turned around and marched right back up that tall hill, but before I had a chance to move, something flashed in the corner of my eye.

I was wound up enough to actually make a small noise of surprise. Wonderful. Delusional *and* dramatic. I was turning out to be your average American, garden variety basket case. And of course the thing that had startled me was the white hound, appearing out of what seemed like nowhere (probably that clump of bushes growing close to the willows) and in front of a large eucalyptus tree that had fallen over recently.

The dog merely stood and stared at me, tongue lolling, eyes twinkling as if he was laughing at me. Great. Even animals thought I was crazy now. We stared at each other, maybe only for a minute, maybe longer. It didn't take long for my patience to run thin.

"Okay dog, I don't know why you led me down here, but if it was to make a fool out of me, you succeeded. Now, if you don't mind, I think I'll walk back home and maybe go back to sleep or get some homework done."

I turned slowly, my head hanging low, muttering to myself as I hunched over against the early morning chill.

"He didn't lead you down here to make a fool out of you," someone said.

Once, when I was twelve or thirteen, my little brothers thought it would be funny to sneak up on me while I was watching a scary movie with my friends during a sleep-over. They waited until the movie was over and we were downstairs discussing the likelihood that some mutated alien would come crashing through my door in the middle of the night to slaughter us all. We ran out of popcorn, and seeing as it was my house, I was volunteered to go upstairs to make more. I expected my brothers to leap out at me once I reached the top of the staircase, and then maybe somewhere else just inside the kitchen when I made it past the staircase unscathed. What I hadn't expected was for my brothers to dress up as aliens and to hide in the pantry. I almost knocked one of Bradley's teeth out and came trainer diapers close to peeing my pants. That was nothing compared to my reaction now.

Obviously, I wasn't expecting the dog to answer me so if I screamed I had good reason to. I just hoped I hadn't woken anybody up in the houses surrounding the swamp. The last thing I needed was for the fire department to show up to rescue the potential murder victim who was just some hysterical high school girl who heard voices. Yes, my classmates would *love* to sink their teeth into *that* information . . .

When my wits returned (well, most of them at least), I shot my head up, grasping my pepper spray so tight I was surprised I didn't accidentally spray myself. There, leaning against a tree, was a young man. He hadn't been there before. I may have a tendency to hallucinate, but I would have noticed him when I first arrived.

He looked relaxed, his arms linked over his broad chest and his legs casually crossed at the ankles. His hair was a dark reddish-brown color and from this distance, his eyes took on a strange, dark shade of green. I had never seen anyone like him in my life. Yet, he was uncomfortably familiar; as if he were one of those people you bump into everywhere but have never officially met.

As soon as my sense of self-awareness returned, my eyes darted around and I swallowed hard. Who was this person? Where had he come from? Did he have anything to do with those crazy gnome things from the other day? Should I run screaming for my life?

"Don't worry, I've taken care of them."

I gaped. *Huh? Who* are *you?!* "Taken care of them?" was what I said instead, as if that were the most important issue at the moment.

"The faelah. They're all gone."

"Faelah?"

The young man grinned and shook his head sheepishly. "I'm sorry, I keep forgetting."

He rubbed the back of his neck and sighed. He looked tired and I wondered what had caused it.

"The small creatures that chased you last week. Humans might call them goblins or trolls."

"Or gnomes?" I offered, and then started in surprise. What was I doing? Taking part in this conversation as if it were normal to stand around on a Saturday morning and chat about imaginary creatures as if they were real. With a strange, albeit, good-looking guy.

"Yes," he said carefully, "or gnomes."

I forgot my timidity and whispered, "You saw them too?"

He nodded. Something about the look he gave me seemed familiar, and once again a snippet of a dream or memory flashed across my mind: this same person, standing before me in the light of the full moon wearing a hooded trench coat.

"Have we met before?" I braved.

He only nodded. "Yes, under unfortunate circumstances."

I waited for him to continue, my fingers all too aware of the small canister of pepper spray in my hand. This was just getting to be too weird.

"You were lured here a week ago, in the middle of the night, and I had to, uh, dispatch a threat."

I felt my knees go weak. That nightmare I couldn't quite remember; the one with the dogs . . . That had actually happened?

At some point I found my voice. "Who are you?"

"I am called Cade." He grinned, but kept his distance.

That struck me as something odd to say. *I am called Cade.* Not, *my name is Cade.* But the name seemed familiar too. "And do you have a last name, Cade?"

He shrugged. "Not one I find much use for."

What on earth did that mean? "Well, I would like to know it anyway."

"MacRoich, Cade MacRoich."

No, I didn't know any Cade MacRoichs. Suddenly another thought hit me. "If I was lured down here last weekend, and all that about those corpse dogs-"

"Cúmorrig," he interrupted.

"Okay," I said, not really caring what fancy name he wanted to give them, "If I wasn't dreaming, why did I wake up in my room?"

Cade grimaced. "I don't think you'll like my answer."

I gestured for him to continue. I didn't think I would like it either, but it seemed important that I know.

"I carried you."

"Okay, thanks for clearing that all up, but I think I'll get back home now."

The last thing I needed was some creepy stalker who broke into my house in the middle of the night, no matter how kind the gesture or how attractive he was.

"Meghan, wait."

I froze and got my pepper spray ready, all the while trying to convince the little hairs on the back of my neck to calm down. I turned, my eyes narrowing even as my heart sped up.

"And just how is it that you know my name?"

He didn't answer. He only stood still as a statue, his dark green eyes studying me carefully. It should have creeped me out even more but it didn't. I worked up my courage.

Revelation

"And how did you get into my room without waking up the entire house?"

"You left the door open when you sleepwalked into the swamp."

Fair enough. "But how did you know where I lived?"

"Fergus showed me."

I glanced over at the grayish-white wolfhound. He had an intelligence about his gaze, but I never heard of a dog who could lead someone to an exact location that wasn't his own home.

I took a breath and relaxed, but only a little. "Listen, I appreciate you helping me the other night, I really do. But this is getting a little too weird for me, and I have too much weird in my life as it is."

I turned to walk away.

"Meghan, did you hear voices growing up?"

I froze. I forgot about why it worried me that he knew my name or where I lived. He could have figured that all out in the past few days by simply paying attention. But to know about my childhood? That was some serious stalking.

"Especially around trees. Did you think they spoke to you?"

His voice was gentle, and even though he moved slowly and carefully towards me, I felt like a rabbit about to spring away from a fox. How could he know this? The sound of the wailing voices and the image of the trees cracking at their bases flooded back to me, the memory blurred at the edges like a water-stained document.

I cried out and stepped back. "Stay away from me," I hissed, the emotion in my voice thick.

"I already know you've seen strange things. Gnomes you called them, and the Cúmorrig. Do you often have nightmares or have visions of things before they happen?"

My head was spinning and it felt like I couldn't pull enough oxygen into my lungs. I stumbled as I took a step back. The golden light of dawn pierced through the trees the way water flowed through a sieve. I didn't care about how beautiful it was. Right then it seemed as if the split sunlight were a thousand probes, searching me out and prying into my mind. *Who are you Meghan Elam?* What *are you?* they seemed to taunt as Cade's questions hit more and more closely to home.

I hadn't realized he had moved closer, and his voice, now a whisper, made me jump.

"And your eyes . . . what color are they?"

I looked up into his, frightened and overwhelmed and enchanted all in the same breath. I could hear his strong heartbeat, though he was careful to keep his distance. His own eyes, I had once decided were a very dark green were now paler, more golden than before. It hadn't been a trick of the light, it hadn't been my miscalculation. They had changed, just as mine changed.

"You see, they were silver when I first met you, but that could have been a result of the moonlight. They were hazel when you arrived fifteen minutes ago, but now they are almost blue. Your eyes change color, of their own accord, don't they?"

And just like that, the spell he had me under snapped. I felt suddenly angry, and terrified. I pushed at his chest and realized it was like trying to move a mountain. Somehow I managed to shove him away, and then I took advantage of his slight surprise and put distance between us.

"Leave me alone!" I shrieked. "You come near me again, you *freak*, and I'll call the cops!"

I bolted, sprinting up the horse path as fast as I could. I still clutched the pepper spray, and I couldn't say why I hadn't used it. That would have slowed him down, surely.

I never heard him come after me and even as I climbed the slope and stumbled onto our shaded back lawn, I didn't look back. It was like the day the gnomes chased me all over again, but this time I was not escaping some horrible little creatures, I was fleeing from an incredibly good-looking guy who could very well

Revelation

understand me completely. I was either saving myself from that serial killer I always imagined lived down in the swamp, or I had finally gone over the deep end.

Ten

Message

or two weeks I ignored what had happened the morning I met Cade for the second time. I never saw him at school posing as the homeless man. It had dawned upon me later that day, once I was safely and securely locked away in my room, that all this time it was him who had been lingering outside my high school. Well, that and the fact that the memories from the night I had wandered into the swamp started surfacing in my mind, like bubbles of wax in my lava lamp. I never ventured outside my house, and I never saw his dog Fergus. It was hard forgetting about what he had said, though. If I had been completely honest, I would have answered yes to each of his questions. I did hear voices, I did see things, and my eyes did change color. But so had his, I was certain of it.

My friends at school noticed my behavior too. Thomas asked me that first week if I had gotten into a fight with my parents. I had looked at him as if he had gone nuts, but he just shrugged and said I seemed even more introverted than usual. After that I tried to act more normal. Well, normal for me at least.

But the truth was, as hard as I tried, I simply could not erase that meeting with Cade MacRoich from my memory. If that was his real name. Who on earth was he? A local college student looking for a little thrill in his life? Some ex-convict with spare time on his hands? And how could he have known about all my

Message

little eccentricities? Even my best friends weren't privy to all my secrets. And why was he so interested in me? I was no one special. It was too puzzling, but I was determined to let it go. I had enough drama in my life.

It was during Thanksgiving weekend that I found the note taped to my sliding glass door. I had kept it locked around the clock and never used it since returning from the strange meeting with Cade. I feared he might try to sneak in and kill me.

At first I thought it was a message from Tully or Robyn, but when I unlocked the door and peeled the note off, I realized the paper was far too ornate to belong to either of them. It was expensive paper, I could tell, and falling victim to my curiosity, I flipped it over. There was an actual wax seal keeping the folded edges shut. I studied the design. An ornate Celtic knot with an eagle in the center. Intrigued, I walked to my desk and fished out my pocket knife, carefully loosening the seal so it wouldn't break. I opened up the letter to find it addressed to me. The writing was impeccable, but not overly ornate. It made me think of a love note that'd been written during England's Georgian period. Hah. Me get a love letter? That would be stranger than fiction.

I began to read and immediately I knew it was from Cade. I had vowed to forget what had happened, but apparently, he hadn't. I should have crumpled it up and thrown it away, right then and there. Or, better yet, I should have taken it straight to my parents and insisted they call the police. Who would have thought that I would ever have a stalker? But deep down, I wanted this mystery cleared up, and the only way to do that was to start by reading the note. Sighing and trying to convince myself nothing bad would come of reading a simple letter, I continued on:

Dear Meghan,

I want to start this letter by apologizing for our last two meetings. As you can tell, I am not at all adept at making proper introductions. Forgive me for not contacting you sooner, but I thought it best to give you some time to let

- 83 -

everything settle in. I wish only to make you aware of two things: who it is you really are, and where it is you come from. I will not go into detail in this letter, for these are not topics which should be discussed in such an impersonal manner. Do allow me, however, to explain our first meeting. You were lured into the swamp, not by myself, but by another who knew of you and who wished to learn more about you. I cannot remember if I explained my presence in the first place, but it was my duty to clear the area around your home of the faelah, and I was unable to finish my job before you arrived. I can only apologize to you again and hope that you might come to forgive me.

Another matter that seemed to disturb you was the fact that I did indeed return you to your residence after you became unconscious after the whole incident. Please believe me when I say that nothing ungentlemanly occurred; I merely wished to see you safe at home, and though you may not believe it, Fergus is a rather clever hound and he did lead the way. On the matter of knowing your name, I must postpone that information until we meet again. I realize this is all shocking to you, but if you try to contact the police, they will not find me. I would not blame you if you did, but you must trust me on this matter.

I will not approach you or seek you out. I shall simply wait until you are ready to learn more. When you are prepared to meet with me again, leave me a note in the hollow knothole of the oak tree along the swamp trail, the tree that is closest to your home. In the mean time, should you find your curiosity unquenchable, I suggest you learn as much about the ancient Celts as you can.

Most sincerely,

Cade MacRoich

I finished the letter and dropped it into my lap, and after a moment I picked it up and read it again. Who wrote letters like that anymore? The language was so, *antiquated.* When I gave it some thought, it dawned upon me that when he had spoken to me in the swamp, he hadn't sounded like he was from this decade, or even this century. It was extremely odd, but then again, I attracted odd the way flowers attract bees.

I glanced up at the blank screen of what used to be my dad's old work computer. So much for forgetting about all that had happened in the past few weeks. I didn't know how long I stared, numb and scared, at that old monitor but at some point in time, three things clicked in my head.

First, whether all this was a hallucination or not, it was happening and I had to address it. No more pushing it aside and hoping it would go away.

Secondly, I had another option. My whole life my only choices with regards to my issues had been therapy and medication. Cade offered a third possibility; that all this was real and that he could explain it all to me. Unlikely and crazy as it seemed, I shouldn't shun it simply because modern society would label me mentally unstable. News flash: I was halfway there already.

And last but not least, I was curious. There, I admitted it. I was one hundred percent, flat out fascinated with what Cade MacRoich had presented to me. Of course, I was terrified as well, but I had always been the type to tackle a good mystery and I was never satisfied with a cover-up story if I felt all the clues hadn't added up.

So, taking a deep breath, I pulled out my binder, flipped to a blank sheet of paper and jotted down the words *faelah* and *ancient Celts*. I was curious, yes, but I was going to go about this the right way. Before meeting with Cade again, I was going to do my research; see how much I could find out on my own. Perhaps I would learn he was the crazy one after all.

I couldn't find much time to research, what with midterms coming up before the winter break, but I did manage to get in a few internet searches and was rather satisfied with the results.

First I searched for the term *faelah*, and of course, nothing came up. I wasn't surprised. I had never heard the word before in my life. Next, I searched for information on the ancient Celts. This proved to be much more promising when a hefty list of websites popped up on the screen. I clicked on one that looked legitimate and was immediately faced with a page full of knot work designs and more lists.

I skimmed the introduction and read the overview. It told me that the Celts were a group of ancient people who inhabited the British Isles and some parts of mainland Europe. They were a tribal people and practiced a pagan religion. Okay, I knew that much from Robyn already. Weird how one of my friends was into this stuff and now I had some guy suggesting I research it. *Just a coincidence,* I told myself.

I clicked on the word *pagan* since it was highlighted, and that took me to a definition. Growing up, I had been led to believe that *pagan* was synonymous with *devil worshipper.* Apparently I had been wrong. I read a few examples, nodding at the list of ancient civilizations that practiced pagan belief systems: the Romans, Greeks, Egyptians, and of course, the Celts to name a few. According to this site, most pagan cultures worshiped a multitude of gods and considered the earth and its bounty to be sacred. That didn't sound too bad at all. In fact, it sounded much like Robyn's own belief system.

I clicked on the link that brought me back to the main page. I looked over the different headings, my eyes halting when I read one that said *Celtic Gods and Goddesses.* I moved my cursor above it and clicked. Once again, I was greeted with a list. I scrolled down the screen, trying to figure out how to pronounce each name as it passed: Balor, the Dagda, Danu, Don, Epona, Lugh . . .

It was when I got to the Morrigan that I stopped. I read it carefully, remembering Robyn's Halloween costume. But something else seemed familiar about the name as well . . .

Cade's voice suddenly played in my mind: "*Cúmorrig. Hounds of the Morrigan . . .*"

I clicked on the name without so much as an afterthought.

The Morrigan: major Celtic deity that is often represented in the three aspects of Neaim, Macha and Badb. She is mostly associated with war and the battlefield and is often depicted in animal form, most commonly the raven.

Message

I stopped reading, my eyes glued to the last word of that sentence. A raven. My mind flashed back to the day I stood waiting for Tully and the afternoon I had cut my finger with the potato peeler. Both times I had seen a raven, too big to be a natural bird. And both times it had watched me, I was sure of it.

My skin prickled and I glanced out my sliding glass door. It was getting late, twilight descending on my backyard like a blanket. I got up and checked to see if the door was still locked. It was. I grabbed the comforter from my bed, wrapped myself in it, and sat back down at my desk. I pulled out my binder, found the section where I had written down my notes from Cade's letter, and quickly jotted down the paragraph about the Morrigan.

Setting my binder aside, I returned to the site's home page. I had read enough about gods and goddesses for the time being. I clicked on the *Otherworldly Creatures* tab. This gave me a list of things with strange names and descriptions: Leprechauns, silkies, fairies, changelings; your usual list. The little creatures that had followed me weren't listed, but a few descriptions from other creatures matched. I decided they either hadn't been prevalent in ancient Ireland, or people's sightings had been sketchy.

Further down the page, I spotted a link that read *familiar animals*. Curious, I opened that link, only to find a Celtic design of several known animals accompanied by a short description. The paragraph above them said that often, animals from the Otherworld were seen by the Celts. Otherworldly animals were very distinctive, and although they were similar to earthly animals in physical makeup, they tended to be larger and white with reddish or rusty colored ears.

My heart thudded in my chest. Fergus. Cade's dog. He was huge, white and had ruddy colored ears. And so did the dog from my childhood memories.

I quickly closed the web page and took several deep breaths. This was too much. It was as if, all my life, I had been puttering around grasping for answers, and they had been just out of my reach. Now, they were here, splayed before me in plain sight. But one big question still remained: what did all of this have to do with *me?* Why was I suddenly surrounded by symbols and creatures from an ancient pagan belief system?

Or worse, I thought, my mouth dry as I tried to swallow, *had these things been around me my entire life, and I was just now noticing them?* The voices, the visions. Had they all been clues and answers trying to break down some invisible barrier?

I had to talk to Cade. I didn't trust him, I didn't know him, but he seemed to be the only one who had any clue about what was really happening to me.

Trying to fall asleep that night was a joke. How could I, what with all I had just learned? I glanced over at the clock, its glowing red letters burning an image in my mind. It was after twelve, but I couldn't sleep. Frustrated, I kicked the sheets back and crawled over to my desk. Ripping a piece of lined paper out of my binder, I wrote:

Cade,

I researched the ancient Celts like you suggested. If you are still willing to help me, I have lots of questions to ask. Can you meet me after school next Tuesday? We get out at 2:30.

Meghan

It was crazy. I was going to ask a strange man to help me answer the biggest mysteries of my life. He could be lying. He could be insane. He could be some sadistic creep who planned to murder me and save my fingernails as trophies. I shivered. As much as my common sense wanted to steer me down a different path, something deeper, something more primitive was fighting to escape the cage I had put it in years ago.

Once the letter was written and I had made the decision to leave it in the oak tree in the morning, I was a little more successful at falling asleep. I thought my dreams would be haunted that night, but instead of the usual goblins and trolls creeping around and cackling at me, I dreamt of a place so beautiful and calm I thought I might weep. I walked through gently rolling country, spongy with damp moss and thick grass. Flowers bloomed everywhere, despite the soft, cool mist that hung in the air. The hills were littered with lichen-encrusted stones, great and small, and in the distance I could see trees that belonged to a very old forest.

I crested one of the hills and it was then that the mist parted and revealed a small, verdant valley and what could only be an old castle, not quite in ruins, nestled against the hillside. It was covered in wild ivy and a sluggish stream trickled past it. Just as the sun was piercing through the fog, scattering its light against the castle's diamond-paned windows, I woke up.

My alarm clock read three in the morning. Sighing, I slouched back into my pillows. I reached up and touched my cheeks. They were wet. Shock coursed through me as I realized I had been crying. But the dream hadn't been terrifying or depressing. As I drifted back to sleep, I realized I had been crying because of the beauty of the place and the knowledge that somehow I knew I had been there before.

The next morning, before school, I slipped through my glass door for the first time in days and crept down onto the wide path leading into the swamp. It was another foggy morning, the cold dewy air rolling over my skin and clogging my lungs. I found the tree almost immediately; the only oak standing amidst the tall, pale-barked eucalyptus on this side of the woods. The knothole was a little harder to find, hidden by a branch and just out of reach.

Once I located it, I glanced over my note once more, rolled it into a tube, and slipped it into the hollow of the tree. Making sure that no one was watching me, I climbed back up the hill, casting my eyes around and listening for Otherworldly creatures. Not until I was safely back inside my room, my door closed and locked behind me, did I wonder once again if I had made the right choice.

Eleven

Rescued

I became obsessed with checking the oak tree for Cade's response. That afternoon when I got home from school, I went down to see if my note was still lodged inside the knothole. It was. An unwelcome pang of disappointment overwhelmed me, but a few mornings later when I checked, it was gone.

Giddy relief flooded my senses, and I had to tell myself it wasn't because my chances of seeing Cade again had just increased. No, I wasn't interested in him. First of all, he was in his early twenties, at least. Even if he wasn't the serial killer my conscience kept trying to paint him as, he was too old for me. Nope, I just wanted to see him again because he might have some answers for me. *But those eyes, dark green at first and as changeable as your own* . . . a tiny voice whispered in my mind. *Ah! Stop it Meg,* I chastised myself, *boys have never been interested in you, remember? Why would this time be any different? And since when have you not been afraid of him? He took on a half dozen of those hellhounds without getting so much as a scratch.*

I shivered, hugging my binder close. It was Friday, only four more days until I was going to meet him again. That is, if he was still willing to meet. I still hadn't received an answer to my letter, and there was still plenty of time to remind myself that Cade

Rescued

MacRoich was closer to being an obsessive stalker than a charming college student I should in no way, shape or form be interested in.

@ @ @

By Sunday morning I had given up on Cade. Maybe I had imagined him after all. I spent some time cleaning my room; doing a load of laundry and picking up the clutter that always littered my floor. I turned on my radio and cranked it up loud so I could hear the music over the vacuum cleaner. It was no surprise then that I screamed when I turned around to find the white wolfhound sitting stoically just outside my sliding glass door. Luckily, Mom had dragged my brothers out shopping for clothes and Dad was at a friend's house watching a football game. Wouldn't want them to think there was anything wrong with me . .
.

I turned down the radio and switched off the vacuum cleaner. I glared at the dog, Fergus, annoyed at his ghostly appearance. It was only after my heart stopped racing that I realized perhaps he was here to deliver a message. I snorted. Yeah right. I had been ignoring this strange, supernatural stuff all my life, why was I welcoming it with open arms now?

Sighing, I walked over to the door, flipped the latch to unlock it, and slid it open. Fergus blinked at me once and opened his mouth to start panting. Cocking an eyebrow, I reached down to pet him. I'd never really tried to pet him before, unless you counted my dreams, and if that was even him in my dreams.

Before my hand made contact with his wiry head, he turned and loped off towards the far edge of the yard. He paused and looked over his shoulder. I was wearing a spaghetti strap tank top and my old ratty sweats. My hair was roughly wrapped in a bun and held there with an old clip. I didn't look my best. Shrugging, I sought out my sandals and slipped my feet into them and grabbed an old sweatshirt on the way out. It was closer to evening than noon, and the late autumn air was chilly. As I walked, I could feel the butterflies fluttering around in my stomach. Would Cade be waiting for me? And I had decided to go out looking like a heathen?

Turned out, I had nothing to worry about. Fergus merely led me to the old oak tree where he proceeded to sit down and whine. It didn't take a brain surgeon to figure out he wanted me to check the knothole. Inside was a note, written on the same type of paper as last time with the same Celtic seal.

Meghan,

Of course I will still help you. Until Tuesday then.

- C.M.

p.s. Keep away from the forest until you see me next.

I couldn't tell you why that simple note made me feel like I was strolling down the beach on a warm summer day. Or, more likely, if I told you the real reason I'd have to go back and re-evaluate my sanity. Let's just say, I was finally going to have some answers, after all my years of fearing to ask them. Yes, that was it.

Fergus escorted me back to my house, not leaving until he heard the lock snap in place on my door. I glanced over my room then turned to look at the white hound with the red ears once again. He was gone. I shouldn't have been surprised. According to my research, he was Otherworldly and probably had oodles of magical abilities. Ah, so I was finally admitting I believed in all this supernatural stuff. Oh well, what else was I to do?

I spent the remainder of the afternoon finishing homework and choosing my clothes for school the next day. Dad got home around five, Mom soon after. She had picked up pizza for dinner, so claiming I still had homework to do, I grabbed a few slices and headed back downstairs. I escaped just in time. My brothers, having endured a day of shopping with Mom, had just unleashed all their pent-up energy from minding their manners all day.

Actually feeling worn out for once, I decided to set my Celtic research aside for one day. Besides, I had an appointment with Cade on Tuesday and I was hoping he would fill me in on anything important I might have missed. A tingle of dread passed through me as I lay in bed, trying to will my mind to calm down so I could fall asleep. The funny thing was, I honestly couldn't tell if my jitters were a result of anticipation at seeing Cade again, or fear that this was all some huge mistake.

I woke up the next morning feeling restless and groggy. I couldn't remember my dream from the night before, but I had a feeling it hadn't been a pleasant one. It took me forever to get ready for school, so Mom ended up taking me on her way to work. The public high school, since it had so many students, started classes at different times throughout the day. Mom's first English class didn't start until later in the morning. This is why I usually got a ride with Thomas or Tully, but on those special occasions when I was running late, Mom was my chauffeur.

"You'll have to catch a ride home with a friend though Meg. There's a teachers' meeting at the high school this afternoon."

I nodded as I pulled myself out of her car in the parking lot of Black Lake High. The final bell had already rung, and I had to visit the office for a tardy slip. I was never tardy to school, so the whole situation put me in a bad mood for the rest of the morning.

At break Tully and Robyn caught up to me.

"Where were you this morning?" Tully asked.

"Slept in," was all I said. It was the truth after all, and I didn't feel like elaborating.

At lunch we met up with Will and Thomas out on the field. To my complete horror and agitation, Adam Peders and Josh Turner were on the opposite end, showing off for a posse of freshman girls. The girls were giggling and falling all over themselves because of the attention they were getting from the two hottest junior boys in the school.

Robyn rolled her eyes and started making barnyard animal sounds. It was the first time I smiled all day. Telling myself to forget about the boys, I sat down with my friends under a tall pine tree and started sifting through my lunch.

Faeloren

Everything was going fine until a familiar voice shouted, "Hey Elam."

I cringed and felt Tully tense up next to me.

Adam sauntered up, his friends following just behind him. *Lemmings,* I reminded myself, trying not to let my fear show. *They're just a bunch of brainless, follow-one-another-off-a-cliff lemmings . . .*

"I heard you were thinking about getting some plastic surgery."

I did *not* want to deal with this today.

"Why, what's wrong with her?" Josh asked, supplying the next line to what I was sure was going to be an insult.

"Someone told me she was born with her ass where her face is supposed to be. But I don't see how fixing it could make a difference."

It was like someone had poured lukewarm bacon grease all over me while kicking me in the stomach at the same time.

I barely registered Robyn jumping up and practically screaming, "Piss off Peders!" or Thomas standing to defend me, only to be shoved back by one of Adam's friends and being fed his very own offensive insult.

Above it all, I could hear the laughter. The freshmen girls giggling and pointing, the other bystanders either shaking their heads in shame or trying to hide their grins.

Suddenly, something inside me snapped. Normally, I would sit in mortification and wait for my tormenters to leave. This time, although I remained sitting, a bone-deep anger began to boil within me. I glared at Adam but he just crossed his arms and simply smirked back, as if to say *'what are you going to do about it?'*

After a silent standoff that lasted a mere few seconds, he snorted and turned to leave, muttering something else to his friends. I didn't hear it this time, but the chorus of chuckles made me believe it wasn't anything pleasant.

"Meg, forget those chauvinist pigs," Robyn was saying.

Rescued

But I wasn't paying attention to her. I kept glaring after Adam, my anger rising. I glanced at the few pinecones scattered on the ground around us, still green and not cracked open by the autumn's heat. I wished with all my might that I could pick up one of those heavy cones and launch it at Adam's head. If only . .
.

I knew right away that my anger must have triggered my imagination, because I pictured one of those cones rising up and flying through the air, making a bee line for the back of Adam's head.

A strange gasp from Tully, and Robyn's shocked face as she pointed numbly at the airborne pinecone, was the only evidence proving that I wasn't imagining anything. The cone cracked against the back of Adam's head and he went sprawling, face first on the dirt track.

My face drained of all color and my heart almost stopped beating. I had killed him. Somehow I had made that pinecone fly through the air and it killed him! For once in my life, I actually felt like I was going to faint. Fortunately, the crowd that had swarmed around Adam backed away and I could see him struggling to sit up. He looked pretty ticked off and when he pulled his hand away from the back of his head, there was blood. He didn't look like he had suffered a concussion, though.

I sighed in relief and almost melted into the grass. I hated Adam, but I didn't want a murder on my hands. It took a few more seconds for my mind to clear, and when it did, it dawned upon me that I had absolutely no idea how I had made the pinecone launch itself at my mortal enemy. Had I really done it? Used some form of telekinetics I unknowingly possessed? I guess it could be true, especially knowing what I'd already witnessed and been a part of this year so far.

"Where did that pinecone come from?" Will asked, his voice breaking into my thoughts.

"Robyn, did you throw it?" Tully whispered.

Faeloren

"No!" Robyn insisted. She gave me a disturbed look, and I merely shrugged, feeling immensely nervous and guilty.

"I'm sitting on the ground. If I had thrown it, the angle would have been greater." Right? I hoped that made sense. I bit my lip. I felt terribly uncomfortable about the whole thing. Besides, I hadn't actually thrown it, and if I did admit it, Adam would probably kill me for making a fool out of him in front of half the school.

"Meghan Elam threw it at Adam, I saw her."

I closed my eyes, wishing for some angel of death to sweep down and take me away.

Robyn hissed beside me. "That *bitch!*"

She sure was laying on the curse words thick today.

Michaela stepped forward with Veronica and Therese, two other girls from the cheerleading squad.

But no one was looking at them. They were all looking at me. I was screwed.

"Come on Meghan," Thomas murmured as he helped me to my feet.

I stood, a little shaky as a result of all the high drama. I didn't know how he thought he was going to protect me. We were sorely outnumbered. And my mom had thought a private school was safer than a public one. At least at a public high school I could have hidden myself in the crowd.

With the help of his friends, Adam stood up and glared so hard at me I suffered from whiplash.

"You are so dead you stupid bitch," he said loud enough only for those closest to him to hear.

I cringed. Should I hope for another pinecone to fly at him? No, that might actually kill him this time.

Before he could make his move, however, the bell signaling the end of lunch sounded shrilly across the campus. At least I could enjoy a few more hours of life before Adam Peders sought his revenge.

Rescued

◎ ◎ ◎

As soon as the final school bell announced the end of the day, I was out of class and sprinting down the hallway like some marathon endorphin junkie looking for the finish line. I had grabbed my books for homework between my last two classes, and now I was on my way to Robyn's car before Adam could find me. It didn't matter that I had not actually thrown the pinecone, and there was no way I could explain what had happened. They already thought I was crazy and the truth would only prove it and give them a reason to do actual harm to me.

I skidded to a stop in front of Robyn's car just as the rest of the student body started trickling into the lot. It took me a whopping two minutes (time I could have used racing to the trail that would have taken me the back way home) to remember that Robyn had a meeting with her Wicca friends today, that Tully had a group science project to work on, and that Will and Thomas had band practice until four. In a sense, it took me two minutes to realize I was a goner.

I cursed and kicked the tire of Robyn's car. I knew she wouldn't take it personally and the only option I had left was to panic. What was I going to do? There was no way on this green earth that Adam was going to let my little infraction slide, and I knew he would enlist his thugs to help him hunt me down. Where were our teachers when you needed them? Ugh, that's what I should have done. I should have ducked into one of the classrooms, feigning confusion on a homework assignment. At least I would have been safe for a while. Now I was merely a sitting duck.

A shout and the sound of my name made me jump. Slowly, I turned my head back towards the school's main building.

I watched Adam and his gang emerge from the hallway, their heads swiveling as they searched me out. It was too late. My friends were preoccupied and I had nowhere else to go; no one to rescue me. If I tried to walk home now, they would follow me and wait until no one else was around . . .

Adam's dark head turned in my direction, and he pointed. My heart leapt into my throat. I started moving again, walking as fast as I could towards the public bus bench. If I was lucky, the bus would pull up and I could get on. I didn't care if it took me further from home, as long as it took me further from Adam Peders. I hopped the bench, and then hurried over to check the schedule. I cursed as tears of true desperation began to form in my eyes. The next bus wouldn't come for another forty minutes. I was doomed.

My attackers drew closer, crossing the parking lot as if it were a field of cheery daisies. My stomach was in knots and my breathing was becoming shallow. It was when Adam was only fifteen feet away that I first heard the growl of an engine. The sound grew louder until it was right beside me, rumbling smoothly.

"Meghan."

I took my eyes off of Adam and his friends, all of whom had miraculously stopped in their tracks. I glanced down and my jaw dropped. It was Cade. He was sitting behind the wheel of a fully restored, classic Trans Am, the silver phoenix emblem standing out against the black paint job. I didn't know a whole lot about cars, but Logan had been really into sports cars since he could walk, and I'd learned a thing or two. The Trans Am would make most car enthusiasts drool in envy.

Cade had removed the t-top, presumably to enjoy the fine weather, and was currently leaning slightly towards the passenger side. I watched in numb shock as he shifted the car into neutral and set the parking break. Then, reaching over, he pushed open the passenger side door.

"Get in," he growled.

Tully and Robyn would have been horrified if they knew I was about to get into a car with some strange guy I had met only twice, and who had admitted to details only a stalker would know. I guess it was a good thing they weren't around for once. The person I had been only a month ago would have been horrified as well. But I was different now, ever since I'd met Cade, and he had insinuated that my visions were not a product of my imagination. No, I still did not trust him. At least not completely. But I had two options to choose from: I could get into the car with him, or I could take my chances with Adam and his knuckle-dragging buddies. I had been wishing for a miracle, and if that miracle exuded danger and mystery and drove a fast car, well, heck, who could blame me if I was grateful? Beggars couldn't be choosers, right?

I glanced back at my tormentors. Adam and his followers weren't looking at me anymore; they were gawking at the Trans Am. *Boys.* I stepped forward and climbed into Cade's car, and that was when the enchantment broke.

Adam stepped forward angrily. "Listen you little slu-"

Cade was up and out of his car so fast I wondered if he hadn't vaporized and somehow reformed just outside his door. Although he stood with his back to the cars whipping by on the highway, his own vehicle acting as a barrier between him and my classmates, he must have looked quite intimidating.

"You no longer have any dealings with Meghan, and if you ever torment or insult her again, I'll be sure to pay you a special visit at your earliest inconvenience."

Something threatening must have showed on Cade's face, because despite his calm voice, Adam paled and nodded his head. Or maybe it was the fact that Cade towered over them.

Adam grabbed his friends roughly and pushed them along, claiming that they had better things to do.

Cade got back into the car, this time at a more normal speed. He closed the door a little too roughly and snapped on his seatbelt.

"Buckle up," he said, his voice hard.

Faeloren

I obeyed, too shocked from what had transpired in the past five minutes to do anything else.

He shifted the car into gear and pulled out onto the highway, gaining speed and heading north. The engine rumbled and the wind tossed my hair over my shoulders. Luckily, it happened to be another one of those ideal fall days, but there was a subtle chill to the air that drew goose bumps from my skin. I pulled my sweatshirt more tightly around me and glanced over at the boy, no, *young man*, sitting next to me.

Cade looked very much the same as he had the last time I'd seen him. He had on a different designer t-shirt, this one a little more fitted than the first one I had seen him in. I caught a glimpse of something metallic circling his neck. I squinted. It looked like a thick braided chain that didn't quite meet up just in front of his throat. It seemed familiar, but at the same time, completely foreign. I shook my head and forgot about it as I studied him further. My eyes lingered on his shoulders then trailed down his arms to find his knuckles white from gripping the steering wheel more tightly than necessary.

I decided he must be a football player. Why else would he be so lean and muscular? Then I remembered that he probably wasn't from this world. It had made me laugh at first, thinking that Cade might not be human. But if I was willing to admit his dog wasn't of this planet, why couldn't I bring myself to believe that Cade himself was from the Otherworld? The Otherworld. The information had been vague on the internet and I hadn't found time yet to visit the local library.

I shook my head slightly and glanced at his face from the corner of my eye. His features were so well-formed, as if he was the final, perfect draft of several failures before. It was during my shameless staring that he decided to flick his eyes in my direction. I felt myself flush. Surely he saw me studying his profile and most likely he thought I was some gawking, moon-eyed teen. Well, I couldn't blame him, I kind of was. I expected him to laugh and make some clever remark about my being attracted to him. Ugh, it would be mortifying. But when he finally opened his mouth, it was to release a deep sigh. His tense stance seemed to melt away, his arms loosened and his knuckles regained some of their color.

"Forgive me Meghan, I'm early. And I shouldn't have spoken so gruffly to you earlier."

I blinked in surprise. Of all the things for him to say, I had not expected that. Yes, he was a day early, but what did that matter when he rescued me from certain death? Okay, that was putting it a little dramatically, but it would have been pretty bad had he not shown up right when he had. Another coincidence? Or had I somehow summoned him as I had summoned the pinecone?

"I wasn't angry at you, but I just finished work less than an hour ago and it oftentimes leaves me a bit rattled. Besides," now he turned and gave me a mischievous grin, "those, uh, *young men*, didn't help improve my mood any."

Interesting . . . I couldn't hear my conscience shouting out its warnings anymore . . . And *young men*? That was putting it kindly.

The wind tossed his dark auburn hair around and he reached up with his left hand to rub the back of his neck. I dropped my gaze for a while and glanced out his window. We were coming up to the top of the Mesa and a quick flash of the view of the Pacific Ocean, held at bay by the pale gold of sand dunes, rushed by. That sight always warmed my spirits, and despite the anxiety I now felt, it had the same effect. I turned and looked in the other direction.

"It's alright. You helped me out, actually," I finally said, my voice subdued.

I felt him more than noticed him stiffen beside me. Could he really be angry at Adam and his friends on my behalf? Suddenly, the butterflies I had felt when reading his notes were back.

To distract myself, I cleared my throat and said, "Why are you early?"

Another sigh from Cade. "I finished my assignment early and I had a feeling you would be needing my help."

"Something to do with Otherworldly senses?" I braved. It was probably a long shot, but it wouldn't hurt to fish a little.

He was quiet for a long while, but eventually he said in a voice as docile as my own, "You could say that."

We both descended into silence after that. We came to the traffic light and turned left to go down the hill, leaving the corner market and the small collection of restaurants behind. As we made it to the bottom of the hill, I took in a great breath and asked, "Where exactly are we going?"

I didn't want to sound suspicious, but as the fear of Adam wore off, my awareness of being in a strange car pushed itself forward.

"To Shell Beach," Cade answered in a clipped tone. "The ocean calms me, and there is a particular spot that is a little more isolated than Pismo."

A shiver ran down my arms and I suddenly had the desire to leap from the car the second we reached the stop sign in the far distance.

"I only wish for isolation because what we are sure to discuss cannot be heard by other ears. The beach is good because there will be other people around, in case you are worried I'm going to try something. And the waves make it impossible for others to overhear. Be calm Meghan, I mean you no harm."

I relaxed, but only a little. Once Cade hit the main part of town, he down-shifted his car and took on a more leisurely speed. The hum of its engine helped soothe my nerves a little. The streets in town were busy with people trying to get their errands done before heading home, so the traffic was more dense than usual. I shot up from my slouched position. I was supposed to have caught a ride home after school.

"What is it?" Cade asked, sensing my unease.

"I have to call my parents. They think I'm going to be home soon."

"When we get to the beach, you can call them. Tell them whatever you need to."

I nodded. I hated lying to my parents but if I told them a classmate and I decided to get together to work on some research after school, it wouldn't be a complete lie. True, I was doing research, to some degree, but Cade wasn't a classmate and I didn't think any of my classes would require asking someone who was potentially from the Otherworld questions about Celtic gods and goddesses.

The spot Cade chose to have our talk was a familiar one to me. The access to the beach itself was along a small road that ran between the edge of a bluff and a charming maritime neighborhood. We both got out of the car and Cade didn't bother locking the doors since the top was off. He offered to put my backpack into his trunk and I nodded in agreement. We headed down the staircase that spilled out onto the gritty sand below. Several more rocks and a half dozen or so sea stacks littered the beach and shore. I liked this spot in particular not only for the huge towers of rock and the tide pools off to the north, but also because the tourists tended to flock to the sandy and pier-adorned Pismo just to the south of this point. I didn't like crowds and to me, long sandy beaches were a bit boring.

There were a handful of people walking below. A husband and wife and their two young sons; an older, fit woman playing fetch with her dog; a young college student and his girlfriend, perched upon a rock, waiting for the sunset. Not so many people that Cade and I couldn't talk and not so few that, if he were to attack me, I couldn't scream and draw their attention. He had chosen well.

Faeborn

Once we reached the bottom of the stairs, I pulled out my cell phone and dialed my home number. To my great relief, Bradley answered the phone.

"Yeah," he said, sounding a little out of breath.

I could hear my brothers screaming and chasing each other around in the background.

"Bradley? It's Meg. Could you tell Mom and Dad I'll be home a little late today? I'm going to be doing some research with a classmate for this group project we have to do."

My brother turned and shouted something at the others, not bothering to cover the phone with his hand. I tried not to grin.

"Meg? Yeah, tell Mom you're going to be late because of a school project, got it."

"Thanks buddy," I said, my shoulders slumping in relief.

"Kay, gotta go. Logan's got a spray bottle and Aiden's supposed to be covering me- Aaaaaagh!"

Chuckling, I hung up. "We're all clear. I have at least two hours I think."

I turned and looked at Cade. My skin suddenly started prickling. He was studying me so intensely I was beginning to wonder if he was of the same opinion as Adam with regards to my face. The recollection of my lunchtime nightmare made my face flame anew.

"What is it?" I asked self-consciously.

He sighed and let his hands drop into his pockets. "Nothing, let's walk. Over there."

He nodded towards the tide pools, the place furthest away from everybody else. I swallowed hard. If I were an ordinary high school girl and if he were an ordinary high school boy, I would be hoping for some romantic liaison on his part right then. But neither of us was ordinary and he was definitely not a high school boy. I had to work hard to get a hold of my wayward imagination. Even if he didn't find me repulsive, it didn't mean he was interested in me in that way. Besides, that line of thinking could get me into trouble.

I paused to take off my shoes and socks. I had this rule about always walking on the beach barefoot. Cade lifted a brow and followed suit. Even his bare feet were attractive. I shook that thought off as quickly as I would a wandering spider. We walked in silence for a while, listening to the waves crash along the shore. I could see why Cade would choose this place to calm his anger. The ocean was soothing; the primitive heartbeat of the earth.

When Cade decided we were far enough away from the other beach goers, he turned and looked at me, his hands still tucked in his pockets. I studied him for a while, still awed by how tall he was. His clothes fit him well and his shoes dangled from the thumb of his left hand. I hadn't noticed his tattoos before; one on each arm, starting near his elbow and twining up to disappear beneath his shirt sleeves. Not surprisingly, they were Celtic in design, intricate, beautiful. It was then that I noticed the bandage on his arm. It wrapped around his wrist and went halfway up his forearm. Blotches of red bled through in many spots.

I darted my eyes up to his, the shock clear on my face. "What happened?"

He took a deep breath and turned his eyes, now a gray-green, towards the crashing waves. "Occupational hazard."

He turned back to me, grinning without showing any teeth. That action turned out to be just as effective as the Mojave sun on an ice cube.

"And, what exactly is your occupation?"

He started in without any preamble. After all, we both had our suspicions of one another. We had both admitted as much those few weeks ago when he had lured me into the swamp and I had taken on his challenge to start my own research.

"I have a duty to fulfill to one who is far more powerful than I. To regulate and control those creatures who don't follow the rules."

I blinked, and not because of the salty spray which had just suffused the air.

"Basically, I am in charge of capturing the Otherworldly creatures that do not belong in this world. Or to punish those who have broken the rules in the Otherworld. I am, in a sense, the Otherworldly Police. Or, if you prefer something a little more dramatic, you could call me a faelah bounty hunter."

I snorted, but not because I didn't believe him. Hadn't I seen him in action that night I had wandered into the swamp in my pajamas? I just thought the term *Otherworldly Police* sounded a bit ridiculous.

"And that is how you hurt your arm?"

He nodded and we fell back into nonverbal companionship.

"I'm sure you have many more questions Meghan. Do not be afraid to ask me, for I intend to tell you more than you probably wish to know."

I swallowed. Hard. That sounded rather daunting. I didn't want to know everything, I knew I didn't, but from the look Cade was giving me, I knew he planned on telling me anyways. Taking a breath, I asked the question that had been bothering me from the beginning: "How did you know my name?"

He cocked his head to the side and smiled. "The internet."

That time I really did laugh out loud. "Seriously?"

He nodded. That was getting annoying.

"It isn't hard to find information on people these days."

"But why did you *want* to find information on me in the first place?"

He ran a hand through his hair. "Your home, Meghan, is very close to a gateway into Eilé, the Otherworld. One I often use because of its convenient location in regards to my home on the other side, and because of how hidden and isolated it is. The scholars and historians call them dolmens, structures composed of rocks, forming a crude doorway of sorts. We Otherworldly folk call them *dolmarehn*. Not too far off the modern term, but if you want to say things properly . . ."

He rolled his shoulders, and I nodded.

"Dolmarehn," I repeated the exotic word, trying it out on my tongue. It sounded creepy, like a word that might be found in a gothic poem.

"It was when I was passing through this dolmarehn that I first detected you. You see, when you spend time in the Otherworld, you absorb its magic. That magic lingers in your system for a while on the other side, here on earth. It wears off in time, almost like a residue, but it gives us extra powers, you could say. Mortals call it glamour. It also gives us the ability to shift our appearance or shape to a certain degree."

An image of Hobo Bob came to mind, hunched over with the face of a very old man.

Cade took a step forward, moving closer. He leaned his arm against the sheer side of the bluff just beside me and looked me in the eye. His were closer to that dark green now and I wondered what color my own eyes were.

"When this residue is still fresh in us, we can easily detect others like us. If the residue is old, then we have to be much closer to each other to recognize one another. You just happened to be passing by on the trail that day." He was quiet now, his voice barely audible over the waves.

"And, and, when was that?" I stammered. I felt like a fool, letting his close proximity bend me to his will.

"Several months ago. I kept an eye on you, did my own research. I was baffled, you see, for you give off a very strong aura, though I suspect you haven't been to Eilé in a very long time. Meghan," he sighed and looked away for a minute, "like me, you are of the Otherworld. You are not human, but immortal. You are one of the Faelorehn."

Twelve

Answers

I think I might have blacked out for a split second, because the next thing I remembered, Cade was holding onto my shoulder as if I was going to fall.

"What?" I whispered, my attention not on him anymore, but fixated on the fascinating shells being washed up by the surf. The grainy sand suddenly felt rough against my bare feet and the underlying smell of fish and salt made my nose sting.

"Here, come sit down a little while," Cade murmured, somewhere a bit too close to my ear.

Unfortunately, I didn't have enough sense to protest. He sat me down on a large, flat rock, its surface warm from the sun, and took a seat next to me. For a while, we just watched the waves, Cade most likely afraid to set me off into a fit of denial or rage, me, well, I was just trying to get a hold of my swirling emotions. Disbelief, for what he had told me couldn't be true. Hilarity because, let's face it, it was ridiculous. And finally fear. I thought, despite everything else, my fear was the strongest.

I couldn't fully accept that what he had said wasn't true, however, for I had seen things with my own eyes and heard things with my own ears that proved the existence of this mythical Otherworld. Just that very day, had I not enticed a pinecone to fly off the ground of its own accord and smash into the back of

Adam's head? But to be a part of it? To have emerged from such a place? To be immortal? I shivered. Despite my violent self-denial, deep down inside I knew it could be possible. After all, I had been found wandering all on my own when I was too young to have true memories, not a scrap of evidence to suggest who I was or how I had ended up in a sketchy section of Los Angeles by myself.

"Do you remember the three questions I asked you, that afternoon in the swamp?"

Cade's words were calm, soothing, as if the simple cadence of his voice could win my trust. It was working.

I nodded, swallowing before speaking, "If I had heard voices or seen strange things, if I had ever had premonition dreams, and," I paused and looked up at him, his now gray eyes calculating, "and if my eyes had a habit of changing color."

He nodded and looked away. "All traits of someone with Faelorehn blood."

I let that digest for a moment, and then asked, "What exactly does it mean to be Faelorehn? And what do you mean, I'm immortal?"

Was it like being faelah? I hoped not. He had called those creepy little creatures that had attacked me and the corpse hounds faelah; surely to be Faelorehn meant something else entirely.

"The Faelorehn are the people of the Otherworld, the books and fairytales would call them fae, or faeries. We look very much like human beings, but as you know our eyes never settle on one color, we have heightened senses of the supernatural, and when we have visited the Otherworld for a length of time, our gifts become stronger in this world. It's almost like a battery Meghan. When we spend too much time here on earth, our powers are drained and we must return to the Otherworld to recharge."

"We?"

Faelorehn

Cade picked up a stone and threw it into the ocean. It went far further than it should have been able to go with the force he had put behind it.

"Yes, *we*. You and I. We are both of the Otherworld; both Faelorehn, both destined to live forever if disease or violence doesn't claim our lives."

I had kind of already surmised that, so it wasn't a surprise to me. I moved on to other questions. "If I'm from the Otherworld, then why am I here? Why did someone abandon me in the middle of Southern California when I was so young?"

Cade cringed next to me. "I have a theory," he said. "I believe you are either the daughter of someone very important and they felt the only way to keep you safe was to send you far away. Or," he paused, casting me a softer look. "Or, you were unwanted, and there was no place for you in Eilé."

Something in that second option must have had some significance to Cade, because he sounded almost pained by it; more pained than he should have sounded as someone simply delivering bad news. I wondered if he had ever been unwanted himself and my heart opened to him.

He sighed. "The only way to tell for sure would be to bring you to the Otherworld and try to discover your origins. But that is not an option right now. It could be dangerous, especially since you have no knowledge of the Otherworld."

"Can you teach me?" I asked, terrified and curious at the same time.

He turned and grinned. "Yes, to a point, but not today. So, tell me what you discovered from your research."

I started out by mentioning Fergus, since his current absence made me think of him.

"I read that Otherworldly animals are white with red ears. But," I thought about the other supernatural creatures; the gnomes, the Cúmorrig, the raven . . . "not all the creatures I saw were white."

Cade nodded. "Fergus is a spirit guide. He is connected to me. Spirit guides are hard to find, but they remain attached to their Faelorehn companion for life. When the ancients saw an animal that was white with red ears, they knew it was Otherworldly because spirit guides are able to do things normal animals can't."

I tucked that information away: white animals with red ears were Otherworldly spirit guides.

I continued to tell Cade what I had learned about the Celts and their deities. He nodded, waiting for me to finish before he spoke again.

"Unfortunately, with our kind not everything is as it seems. The Otherworld is very similar to this one, parallel you could say, but on a different dimension; linked together but not dependent upon one another. We have plants and animals and everything you might find here, but our people are capable of shifting between the worlds. The Faelorehn and the faelah can come and go between this earth and the Otherworld, but human beings and the other denizens of this planet cannot enter our world."

I nodded, letting him know I still followed.

"Long ago, our people first discovered a way to enter into this place, through the dolmarehn. Many were built, both here and in our world. We discovered the relative weakness of humans and unfortunately, the most powerful of our kind exploited that weakness. They are the ones who cannot be killed, and they became gods and goddesses to the ancient people of northern Europe."

This made sense, if any of it could make sense. I had seen science specials on TV that tried to claim aliens were responsible for building the pyramids, so why couldn't the Faelorehn have slipped into our dimension and impressed early humankind with their supernatural strength?

"Someday I'll show you the dolmarehn that I most often use, but not today. The Otherworld is a dangerous place Meghan,

Faeforegn

even to one who belongs there, and if you don't know what to expect, it can kill you."

That sounded daunting. The small bits and pieces of the Otherworld I had seen in this world were terrifying enough. I nodded severely, letting Cade know I concurred. The last thing I wanted to do was go wandering around in a strange place full of various faelah.

Cade was silent for a few seconds, then he turned and looked at me. His skin took on the golden hue of the sun as it fell further towards the horizon. Some well buried instinct tried to coax me into reaching out and touching him, but fortunately my better sense squashed it before I made a fool of myself. Honestly, what had gotten into me?

"Are you well?" he asked.

I screwed my face up into an expression of confusion. Had he known what I had just been tempted to do?

"With all of this, I mean. I have just told you that you are a being from the Otherworld, that you do not truly belong here."

I simply nodded, unable to come up with a good response.

He shrugged. "Some people would not take it as well as you seem to be taking it."

"No," I finally managed, "it's a shock. To be honest, I don't think it's quite settled in yet. I still expect to wake up from some strange dream." I grinned and cast him a sideways glance. "I have lots of those, you know. Strange dreams."

He smiled and seemed to relax a little.

We watched the sun set before we got up to leave. The young couple was still there, but everyone else had left. As we headed back up the Mesa, I thought long and hard about what Cade had said. It made sense, in a perverse, twisted universe sort of way. If anything, it explained all the visions I'd had and all the voices I'd heard my whole life. The upside: it meant that I wasn't crazy. The downside: it meant I wasn't human. The mere thought made me light-headed. I wondered if I could come to accept that.

Answers

Cade's Trans Am rumbled up to the front of my driveway just as twilight was settling in. He put the car in neutral and got out to open the trunk. He handed me my backpack.

"I'll be in touch," he said. "There are a few errands I have to do; a few things I need to take care of in the Otherworld." He ran his hand through his thick hair again. A habit, I was beginning to realize, when he was worried about something. I found it endearing.

"We'll talk more about this when I return. Don't be afraid to use the oak tree again, and I'll ask Fergus to keep an eye on you."

I smiled, a warm glow spreading through my stomach.

Cade climbed back into his car and closed the door. "Oh, and Meghan," he said, calling out to me through the passenger side window, "one other thing you should know,"

"What's that? I'm a long lost princess?" I joked as I hiked my backpack up onto my shoulder.

Cade grinned and shook his head, "No."

I waited. Finally he took a deep breath and spoke, his voice hardly audible over the rumble of his idling car, "Stay away from the swamp as much as possible, and don't trust anyone who claims to be Faelorehn."

He gripped the steering wheel and gazed straight ahead, past the broken barbed wire fence and the sign that read *Dead End* where our street met the horse path several yards away. "They know about you now, and I don't yet know what they might want with you."

I blinked, wanting very badly to ask him a dozen more questions, but he'd been sitting there for a while and his car was loud enough to draw attention from inside the house. The last thing I needed was a barrage of questions from curious family members.

He reached into his pocket and pulled out something attached to a thin leather string. He threw it through the window and somehow I managed to catch it.

Faelorehn

"Keep that on your person at all times," he said.

I examined it. It looked like a wooden bead with some sort of ancient rune burned into it. "What is it?"

He smiled again, "Mistletoe."

I arched my eyebrow at him. Was he flirting with me? I felt my face flush.

"We Faelorehn use it to ward off evil spirits. The same way some people might wear garlic to frighten off vampires."

Nodding, I slipped it around my neck and tucked it under my shirt.

"Goodbye for now Meghan. When I get back, I'll tell you more of what I know and perhaps even teach you how to defend yourself against the faelah."

I took a step back and he shifted into gear. I watched for a while as his dark car disappeared around the first bend of our road, and listened until I could no longer hear its soothing rumble. Sighing, I walked up our short, sloping driveway and tested the front door. It was unlocked. The house was noisy as usual, with Mom making dinner and the boys attempting to do their homework, but failing miserably.

"There you are!" Mom proclaimed after testing the marinara sauce she had on the stove.

"Yeah, sorry. We had more research to do than I thought," I lied.

"Uh huh," she said, giving me a rather knowing look.

Confused, I said, "Bradley gave you my message, right?"

"Oh, yes, he gave me the message, but," she cast my father a glance. He was engrossed in the local news station, so she looked back at me, smiling. "I'm not surprised your research took longer than expected. From what I saw, I can't say I blame you."

For about ten seconds I was completely flabbergasted. What on earth was she talking about? Then I glanced through the window over the sink and realized that she had had a clear and unobstructed view of our driveway. I turned beet red.

"No, but, we really . . ." I stammered.

My mom laughed, then grabbed my elbow and pulled me deeper into the kitchen. "Oh come on! He was cute. What's his name?"

"Mom," I grumbled, completely mortified and eternally grateful my brothers couldn't hear us, "we were studying for an English assignment, really. It's not what you think."

Oh, if only she knew how far off the mark she was. But I couldn't tell her any of what Cade and I had discussed. She wouldn't believe me and it would only lead to more treatments for my insanity.

"Okay honey, if you insist." She winked and I grumbled something about more homework on my way downstairs.

I tried to get my homework done, I really did, but I couldn't stop thinking about everything Cade had told me. How did one come to terms with the fact that they weren't human? And what if I had been abandoned, unwanted by my real parents? Although my family loved me dearly, and I loved them, there was something painful about the knowledge of being cast aside by those who had created you to begin with.

I shivered. Maybe I had been wanted and had been sent to this world for my own protection. But if so, why had there not been a note of explanation and why hadn't anyone come to find me and tell me? No, I was sure I had been unwanted, for my birth family would have sought me out by now and I wouldn't have been discovered by some random Faelorehn guy tripping over me while trying to do his job.

Mom called down to tell me dinner was ready, and doing my best to compose myself, I went up and joined my family, feigning normal once again. I was good at it, after all.

That night as I lay in bed, contemplating the shambles that was currently my life, I wondered when I'd see Cade again. He had dropped a bombshell on me; there was no doubt about it. Immortal? Otherworldly? It was too mind-boggling to consider.

Faeloren

I couldn't even imagine living for all eternity. The very though scared the crud out of me.

As the sounds of the day wound down and the silence of night fell over me, my mind continued to whir in thought. I needed to know more, so much more. I felt like a beginning swimmer, thrown into a stormy sea infested with sharks, barely able to keep my head above water. I pulled the mistletoe bead from beneath the old t-shirt I had put on before bed. The rune that was burned into the surface of the smooth wood was black and harsh, but it felt warm in my hand. Sighing, I tucked it back away, wondering if I would see more faelah the next day.

After hours of tossing and turning, I finally fell into a troubled sleep, terrified of what the future might hold. High school was hard enough, but I couldn't imagine what it was going to be like now that I knew I was definitely not like everybody else.

Thirteen

Attacked

A week passed before anything bizarre happened, and even then it wasn't much. Cade had stayed away like he said he would. I hadn't even seen him posing as Hobo Bob in the mornings or afternoons. Even when I happened to glance up from my homework in the dark of night, hoping to spot an enormous, ghost-like dog just outside my door, I was left seething in my own disappointment.

That was when I would remind myself that my only interest in Cade was purely an educational one: he knew the answers to my lifelong questions, and I simply wanted to know what those answers were. *Doesn't help that he's built like a pro athlete,* a voice in my head whispered. *And he seemed pretty interested in you, if you ask me.*

Don't listen Meghan, another voice said, *you can't trust him. How do you know he isn't making up all this Otherworld nonsense in order to pull the wool over your eyes?*

Then the voices started to argue and I threw my math book across the room in frustration. It was a pretty bad sign when the voices inside your head started fighting with one another. I'm not sure what degree of crazy that made me. Regardless of what tricks my conscience was playing on me and whether I believed Cade had an ulterior motive or not, I needed to leave all options open until I had definite proof of what was true and what wasn't.

School that week was the same as it always was: the slow, grueling gauntlet all teenagers are forced to crawl through in order to pass on to adulthood. I was really quite surprised to learn that Adam and his friends seemed to be taking Cade's words to heart. I half expected to open my locker Tuesday morning and find some ominous threat, but as the week progressed, the worst I got from him and his cronies was a rude hand gesture or a nasty scowl. Sometimes I imagined they were planning revenge; quietly waiting until all signs proved that the guy with the black sports car was gone for good. Now I had another reason to wish for Cade to come back.

It was on my ride home the following Monday, exactly one week after my talk with Cade, that I noticed the raven again. Robyn was dropping me off at my house and my mind was still too caught up in thoughts of my unusual identity and the young man who had revealed it to me to notice anything out of place.

"Hey Meg, what're you doing Saturday?" Robyn asked through the passenger side window.

I shrugged. "Sleeping in hopefully."

"Want to go to the old post office in Halcyon with us? We were thinking about getting some Christmas shopping done."

I thought about it for a moment. The Halcyon post office was one of our local hidden gems, an old mail building turned gift shop from when the town was first established about a hundred years ago. Although it still functioned as a post office for the small community of Halcyon, it also offered an eclectic collection of incense, chimes, home-crafted jewelry and apparel, independent books and, to Robyn's delight, plenty of artifacts that appealed to her more unique tastes. *And,* I thought as Robyn awaited my answer, *it will give me a chance to do something other than wonder when Cade is coming back . . .*

Attacked

I shrugged my backpack further up onto my shoulder. "Sure. What time were you thinking about going?"

"We'll pick you up at ten."

I grinned and waved Robyn on, watching as her car puttered around the corner. It was then that I spotted the raven out of the corner of my eye, sitting on a high eucalyptus branch. If I hadn't known any better I would've sworn it was whispering to something clinging to the side of the tree. Wait, I *did* know better. The raven was from the Otherworld, I knew that for certain. That meant it was at least as intelligent as Cade's dog. A memory surfaced then, something I had read during my research. Something about the Morrigan and ravens . . . Ah, that was it. One of the Morrigan's symbols was a raven. Could this bird belong to a Celtic goddess? I snorted. Now *that* was a stupid thought. That would mean that a goddess was interested in me. No, it just had to be another Otherworldly creature, drawn to my Faelorehn presence.

Doing my best to drive away my sudden nervousness, I narrowed my eyes and watched the large bird. The creature it 'spoke' to looked somewhat like a squirrel, but its tail was more like a rat's and its face was, in a word, grotesque. Strange, I didn't even notice that it was bright red until after I observed those other details.

I blinked and suddenly found two sets of eyes upon me; the raven's dark red ones and the demented squirrel's yellow ones. Shivering, I clutched my binder and spun on my heel, walking up my driveway as swiftly as possible.

I didn't see any other strange Otherworldly things for the rest of the week and on Saturday morning Robyn pulled up in her small car with Tully.

"Where are Thomas and Will?"

"Band practice," Robyn answered with a sniff.

I smiled and climbed in the back with Tully.

Faeborn

"What am I, your chauffeur?" Robyn asked as she twisted around to look at us.

I smiled. "Yup."

"Whatever."

Tully laughed as Robyn hit the gas. She always drove too fast. We never said anything to her about it because the last time we did she got mad and drove faster. If it hadn't been for the speeding ticket she'd received five minutes later, I'm sure she would have forgiven us by the end of the day. Instead, she spent a whole week giving me and Tully the cold shoulder. It was a really calm week.

Robyn pulled onto Highway One and quickly bypassed the speed limit as we headed into town. She pushed a CD into her car stereo and soon we were listening to the shrill screech of the latest punk band she was into. Ten minutes later we pulled into the quiet dirt parking lot of the tiny post office. I stretched my back once I was out of the car and eyed the newest stained-glass peace sign hanging from the store's window. I smiled. It would be nice to have a weekend jaunt with my two best friends that didn't involve running from faelah or stressing over an identity crisis. Of course, the day was still young.

I looked back towards the store, seeking a distraction from my wayward thoughts. The post office itself was a minute, old Victorian home that had seen its share of wear and tear. It was painted brick red with a large wooden sign bearing its name written in a dated script perched above the door. A set of concrete steps stood in place of a wooden porch and a planter full of exuberant succulents spilled onto the walkway.

We shuffled our way to the front door, an elderly lady giving us a kind grin and mumbling something about 'darling girls' as she walked past. When she saw Robyn, however, she stopped and stared. Robyn, in her old army boots, black fishnet tights, tattered mini jean skirt and t-shirt featuring a skull and cross bones, only

Attacked

made a face and flashed a popular rock and roll hand gesture as the poor old woman gave her a wide berth.

"Robyn, do you have to be so crass?" Tully hissed as the tiny bells hanging above the door jingled.

"Oh come on!" Robyn snorted. "If you are going to shop at this store, then you shouldn't be shocked to see a genuine pagan just outside of it!"

"You're not a genuine pagan," I said without thinking.

Both Robyn and Tully stopped and looked at me as if I had sprouted mushrooms all over my face. But I couldn't blame them. Out of everyone in our small group of friends, the boys included, I was probably the one who was the least interested in Robyn's 'religion'. Sure, I went to her celebrations and took part, but everyone knew it was only for Robyn's sake that I did it. Of course, that was all before I had met Cade, done my research on the Celts or learned that I was one of the Faelorehn . . .

Robyn crossed her arms and gave me her most condescending look. "Come again?"

I took a deep breath, getting a good sampling of the eighteen thousand types of incense the cashier had burning, and shrugged my shoulders. "I was just kidding. Jeesh, don't be so sensitive."

Robyn shrugged and headed to where the crystals were located, but Tully stuck by me. To my great relief, no one dug further into my bizarre remark.

We spent a good thirty minutes poking around the dusty little store. I made sure to look at everything, in case I found something my brothers might like. I didn't think any of them would be interested in Tarot cards, glittering statues of fairies or books on how to find your inner Chi, but I did find a nice pair of amethyst earrings that my mom would love.

At some point in time Tully decided to join Robyn in the crystal section of the store and I wandered back over to the books. I wasn't looking for anything in particular, just wasting time until my friends were ready. As my eyes passed over the spines of the books, they froze on one title in particular: *Irish Folktales*.

Looking up to make sure Robyn and Tully were still distracted in the opposite corner, I slid the book out and flipped to the table of contents. A list of stories, all having names that looked impossible to pronounce, glared back at me. A few of the names I recognized from what Cade had told me and from what I had seen on my website search. I closed the book and looked at the cover. I almost dropped it as my heart leapt into my throat. A few months ago, I would have thought nothing of it. I would have admired the fine Celtic knot work before returning it to the shelf. But this image seemed too familiar to me. It was a stone carving of what looked like a wild man, and at his side was a wolfhound. Cade and Fergus came immediately to mind and I hurriedly flipped back to the copyright page to see who the image depicted.

Cuchulainn was all it said. Cuchulainn? That name didn't look familiar. I would have to check those sites again and make a note to visit the library.

I closed the book and looked up to see what my friends were doing. Still distracted by the crystals. Good. As nonchalantly as possible, I slinked over to the cash register where a tall lady with fading strawberry blond hair looked up at me over her glasses.

"Hello there, all ready?"

"Sure," I said as quietly as I could.

If Tully and Robyn saw me purchasing a book on Irish myth, I wouldn't be able to brush them off so easily. I would have to explain to them why I would want such a book. I decided early on, when my life started barrel-rolling out of control, that they wouldn't know about who, no, *what*, I was unless absolutely necessary.

The woman slipped the book and the amethyst earrings into a bag as I nervously drummed my fingers against the glass counter. When she gave me a questioning look, I smiled and forced my fingers to stop. Instead, I pretended to admire the knickknacks that sat locked away beneath the counter. I paid the lady, then stuffed my bag into my purse and walked over to Tully and Robyn.

"You guys done?"

"Yeah, I think I'll wait on the crystals," Robyn said.

Tully lifted up a stained-glass candle holder. "Think I'm going to get this."

Before either of them could ask my opinion, I said, "Okay, I'll just wait outside if it's alright with you two."

They shrugged and I headed straight for the door. A few minutes later they joined me in front of Robyn's car.

"So did you find anything for your brothers?" Tully asked.

Drat. "Um, nope. But I found some nice earrings for my mom."

"Oh really, can I see?"

Double drat. "Hang on."

I turned away as I rifled through my purse. I slipped my hand into the bag and managed to remove the small box without removing the book with it.

"They're amethyst," I offered with a grin, relieved that my new book would remain a secret.

As my friends admired the earrings, I cast a glance at the old walnut trees growing in the vacant field next to the store. I half expected to see the raven again or some other creepy crawly, Otherworldly thing, but luckily the only thing I saw was a calico cat sitting patiently over a gopher hole.

Tully handed me my box and we piled back into Robyn's car. I opted to sit in the front seat this time.

"I didn't get any Christmas shopping done in there," Robyn griped. "How about a trip into town?"

"Sounds good to me," Tully offered.

Robyn arched a black eyebrow at me. I shrugged. "Hey, I have five brothers and the only thing they want for Christmas is candy, video games and toys. Can't get any of those things at a local gift shop that caters to the spiritual crowd."

"Okay, town it is." Robyn grinned and pulled back out onto the road.

The rest of the day passed by in a whirlwind of store hopping, lunch at a local diner and an afternoon spent lazing in the park in Arroyo Grande's old village square. The Village was probably one of the most popular hangouts for those who attended both the local public high school and Black Lake High. With its diverse collection of old vintage shops, a café, an old-fashioned ice cream parlor and plenty of mom and pop restaurants, it was the place to waste time on a nice winter afternoon.

When we'd had enough of lying around in the sun, Tully, Robyn and I crossed back over the Village's famous swinging bridge to the side street where we had parked. The cables creaked in protest as we crossed over the small canyon the Arroyo Grande creek had carved out, and when I reached the middle of the bridge I paused to look over the edge. I had always had slight acrophobia, but I felt secure enough to lean against the edge of the bridge and peer over.

"C'mon Meg!" Robyn called out from the other end. "I promised my mom I'd babysit tonight!"

Letting loose a sigh of contentment, I moved to straighten from my bent position. Unfortunately, I never got as far as fully standing up. Three things happened at once. First, I heard Tully and Robyn screaming my name and telling me to watch out. Secondly, I remember hearing them and registering that they were concerned about something. And the final thing I remember before nearly being thrown over the side of the bridge was the presence of some great shadow just behind me.

The shadow slammed into me with a force equivalent to a football player intent on tackling me. Yet, it didn't feel like it had made contact; it was more like the force of a shockwave spreading over me. It made my ears ring and I had definitely felt it, but it hadn't been enough to throw me over the bridge. Tully and Robyn were screaming, my shoulder and the left side of my body felt like it had been beaten with a baseball bat, and my fingers hurt from clinging to the chain link railing of the safety fence of the swinging bridge. I felt dizzy, confused and terrified all at once. Only when I heard a low, angry grumble did I think to look up. Blinking away my fear, I just caught a glimpse of a huge black shape as it disappeared into the canopy of the trees lining the creek.

My stomach lurched. No, it couldn't be . . . But another harsh, angry caw confirmed my suspicions. The raven. Had it just tried to *kill* me? Why? For what purpose?

The pounding of Robyn and Tully's feet as they came running up to me sent all my questions scattering away. I would definitely be talking to Cade about this. That is, if I ever saw him again.

"What the *hell* was that?!" Robyn breathed as she tried to find the raven in the treetops.

"Come on Meg, let's get off this bridge." Tully was pulling on my arm, but my weak legs were having trouble moving.

"Was that a crow? A vulture? It was way too big . . ." Robyn was saying as she hurried along behind us.

"I don't know," I barely managed as I clutched my shoulder. It hurt where the raven had hit me, but already the pain was fading away.

We made it to the car in record time.

"Whatever it was, it looked like it was trying to knock you over the bridge," Tully muttered.

I shrugged. I knew that was exactly what it had been trying to do. For weeks the bird had been spying on me and now that I knew Otherworldly beings, faelah, existed, I had no reason to second guess my first instincts. But there was no way I was going to tell my friends.

"Let's just get home before we're attacked by any other mutant birds."

I nodded my agreement and soon we were heading back towards the Mesa, silent in thought the entire way.

That evening I made sure my sliding glass door was locked before I went to bed. As I tried to get myself to fall asleep, I sent up a secret prayer that Cade would come back soon and teach me how to defend myself against the supernatural creatures that for some reason or another, wanted me dead.

Fourteen

Smitten

The winter break came swiftly and as the weather grew cold and wet, I found myself spending much of my time indoors with my brothers, most often playing their video games or some of the board games we had stored away. Ever since that day in the Village, I had been reluctant to spend any time outside. Cade still hadn't indicated he was back from his business in the Otherworld, and until I had someone who could show me how to avoid being annihilated by some demented, supernatural demon, I was going to stay out of their way.

When I wasn't distracted with my brothers, I was down in my room, reading through the book I had found at the store in Halcyon. It turned out that Cuchulainn was some sort of godlike hero from ancient Ireland who was famous for outsmarting and outplaying his opponents during any challenge. He made me think of some sort of Celtic version of Hercules or Achilles. Although the book provided me with an interesting read, it wasn't the best source for the information I sought. Even my few visits to the local library proved fruitless. It was time I got back to my internet searches.

I spent my mornings and sometimes my evenings reading everything I could find on the Celts, and especially the Otherworld.

Faelorehn

One site informed me that the people of Ireland considered caves, hills and lakes to be portals to the Otherworld. That got me thinking about the dolmarehn Cade had told me about. I scrolled through another few sites, all of them telling me the same things over and over again. I already knew the Celts were a tribal culture, that the druids acted as their priests and performed the pagan rituals; that they believed the barrier between our world and the Otherworld was more permeable on Samhain. I had already read all of this before. What I wanted to know was what was it like in the Otherworld? What sort of abilities did the Faelorehn possess? And most importantly, why did it seem like the faelah were after me and what could I do to defend myself?

Cursing silently, I closed the page I was on and crossed my arms in a huff. Research was leading me around in circles. I wasn't going to learn anything new or relevant. What I needed was a nice long conversation with Cade. Where was he? What was taking him so long to get back to me? My frustration was growing worse by the day, and soon I was going to go crazy locked up inside the house, afraid to leave in case the faelah were waiting just outside the door.

The next morning, I woke up early and padded over to my sliding glass door. This had become a habit of mine, and every morning I hoped to see some sign of Cade's return. The oak tree was just visible over the edge of our yard and as I traced the outline of its trunk in the gray light of pre-dawn, a shape stepped out from behind it. I nearly jumped through the glass in my surprise. *Fergus!*

I threw on a sweatshirt, unlocked my door and slid it open without a second thought of ravens or faelah waiting for me in the shadows. I slipped on some sandals and hurried down the slope that led to the tree.

Fergus released a small bark and pressed his front paws against the trunk of the oak tree. I felt like hugging him, but my eagerness at finding a note from Cade outweighed my joy at seeing his dog. His *spirit guide.*

I hurried over and pulled the parchment out of the knothole. With nervous fingers, I unrolled it.

Meghan,

Now that you've had adequate time to allow the truth of who and what you are to sink in, I feel you are ready to meet with me again. Please join me in the clearing tomorrow morning if you are able.

Sincerely,

C.M.

I read it again, twice, and then clutched the note to my chest. Fergus released a small whine and I looked down at him, blushing like an idiot. He eyed me curiously, that strange intelligence of his sparkling in those brown eyes. Could he somehow relate my behavior back to Cade? I hoped not. I folded the note and stuck it in my back pocket, whistling all the way back to my house.

There was a light rain the next morning, but I wasn't going to let the gloomy weather keep me from my plans. Finally I was going to see Cade and finally I should get some more answers. After grabbing a quick breakfast and fending off my attention-seeking brothers, I told my parents I was going for a walk and headed out the door.

"Where are you going in this weather?" my dad asked.

I froze. "Um, just down into the swamp."

Mom furrowed her brow and looked up at me over her magazine. "The swamp? Since when have you enjoyed going down there?"

I cringed. I never showed any true interest in it before, so her question was a legitimate one. "Since I spotted some neat trails on my way home from school once," I responded, cringing at my fabricated reasoning.

Both my parents looked at me as if I had gone crazy. Well, *crazier.*

"Hiking trails?" they both said together.

"Yeah," I waved my hand around, the sleeve of my lime-green rain jacket flapping against my wrist, "it's really nice down there. You should check it out sometime."

My parents looked slightly baffled, but they both shrugged it off and got back to reading their magazines.

"Okay, well have fun honey and be careful," Mom finally said.

Hardly believing I made it out of that one with my intelligence intact, I scurried through the front door and walked down to the road. I squeezed past the *Dead End* sign and began my descent into the swamp. I made sure I could feel the can of pepper spray in my pocket and kept my senses alert. Halfway to my destination it started raining again. Most of the moisture was caught and stopped by the eucalyptus trees above, but by the time I had the clearing in my sights, rain drops speckled my raincoat like chicken pox.

Cade was waiting for me, Fergus standing loyally beside him. My heart skipped a beat and I had to squash my sudden nervousness. What was wrong with me?

Cade had on the black trench coat I remembered from before, hood flipped up. He had what looked like two walking sticks in one hand and a couple of long pouches in the other. As I moved closer, I noticed that the pouches had feathery branches sticking out of them. No, not branches: arrows. I eyed the staves he was holding. A long string looped around the top of each of them and trailed loosely to the ground. Oh. Bows. I thought bows were supposed to be curved . . .

I'm sure the look I gave him held puzzlement, because he smiled. He had smiled at me before, that time at the beach when he told me what I was and a few times before that, but I had never noticed the small dimple before. Suddenly, my legs felt slightly weak and I forgot all about my irritation at his long absence or all those questions I was going to ask.

Smitten

I cleared my throat and pointed at the bows, taking my eyes away from his. "Um, shouldn't those be curved?"

Cade laughed lightly and it didn't do anything to help my posture. Cursed, weak legs . . .

"They will be," was all he said.

He set the quivers and the smaller bow aside and abruptly placed the stringed end of the bow against one foot, passing it behind his other leg. Then, using his right leg for support, he bent the bow and slipped the other loop into place. When he stepped out of the bow, it looked the way it should.

"The wood is what gives it its flex."

He demonstrated by pulling the string back but not releasing it. "The strongest yew wood available."

It was rather impressive, I had to admit.

"So," I said, clearing my throat, "you called me down here to play Robin Hood? Because I actually had a few questions for you, well, more than a few, but what I need to know most is why am I being stalked by a raven that wants to kill me?"

The light in Cade's eyes faded and his jaw tightened. He nodded infinitesimally and sighed. "I know about the raven and what happened on the bridge," he said, "that's why I've brought the bows. We're starting your training right away."

Training? But I was more curious about how he knew about the raven, so I asked him.

Cade merely shot a quick glance at Fergus. Ah, so maybe he could communicate telepathically with his dog. But how had Fergus known? Had he been following me too? I decided that at this point, it was probably best just to believe anything was possible.

Cade leaned his own bow up against a tree and reached for the smaller one, apparently done with the Q and A portion of our conversation. "It is much more convenient to fight any faelah creatures when you can pick them off from a distance."

He handed the bow out to me, smiling again as he did so. He really needed to stop doing that. I figured I was going to have a hard enough time stringing the bow. It wouldn't help if my legs were perpetually turning into jelly.

Cade showed me how to string and unstring the bow and although it was a struggle, I managed on my own after awhile. He had to step in close to me for the first several times and although his closeness made my heart beat in my throat, I won't say I didn't enjoy it.

After our bows were strung, Cade pulled out two pairs of special gloves he told me should always be worn when practicing archery. Mine were much smaller than his, but they fit me perfectly.

"Now, the arrows that we'll be using are practice ones. I'll bring you some rowan wood arrows next time."

"Rowan wood?"

Cade nodded as he nocked one of his arrows. "Rowan helps ward against evil."

I nodded. I guess I hadn't done enough research after all.

Silence followed Cade's explanation as he focused and drew his bowstring far enough back that the feathers of the arrow brushed his cheek. He must have come early because about a hundred yards away I noticed an old piece of cloth pinned against a grassy berm, its center painted with a red and white target.

I waited patiently as Cade breathed deeply, focusing on his task. Fergus panted beside us and the light rain had become an annoying drizzle. Finally, Cade released the arrow and the bowstring splattered moisture on both of us. The arrow flew straight, whooshing through the air and lodging deeply into the center of the target.

I felt my jaw drop. *That* was impressive. I looked at Cade, my eyes wide, but he merely gazed at the distant target, his face looking slightly grim as he nodded once and reached for another arrow.

"You will not always have that much time to focus on your target, so it is important that you learn to shoot quickly."

I gaped at him. That was it? No smile or grunt of approval? If he had been any of the jocks at my high school he would be crowing as loudly as he could, trying to draw the attention of every female within a mile radius to come see his impressive feat of masculinity. But Cade wasn't like those guys at school. No, he wasn't like them at all . . .

"Meghan?"

I snapped out of my daydream. "Huh?"

"Are you ready to try?"

"Uh, yeah." I bit my lip and gripped my bow. *Time to focus Meghan. You don't want to end up shooting your new friend or yourself in the foot.*

Cade handed me an arrow, then shocked me by stepping behind me and putting his left hand on my forearm and his other hand over the one I was using to grip the bowstring. I swallowed and forced myself to breathe through my nose. He could easily rest his chin on the top of my head if he wished, and I almost thought he was going to.

"Now," he murmured, just loud enough for me to hear him.

He was so close I could feel the vibration of his voice in his chest; the heat coming off his body. I gulped down my nervousness.

"Nock the arrow first and use your left hand, the one gripping the bow, as a rest for the arrow. Your glove will protect your hand. Hook your first three fingers over the string, keeping the nock of the arrow between your index and middle finger."

Carefully, he used his own hands to guide mine. His touch was gentle, but reassuring, and it took every fiber of muscle in my legs to keep my knees from buckling.

He tightened his right hand over mine.

"Now, draw the string back as far as you can. For now, don't draw it all the way to your cheek."

Faeloren

Cade pulled the string back with me, only bringing it to a point just in front of my nose. As I waited for his next instruction, I took advantage of his close proximity. Although he didn't quite touch me, I could feel his presence mere inches away from my back. The pleasant earthy scent that always accompanied him filled my senses and the rhythm of his calm breathing almost kept pace with my heartbeat. Unfortunately, my heart was trying to run a marathon right then.

"Keep your arms steady and keep a hold of the arrow."

Slowly, he released my arm and hand, backing away to leave me standing on my own. A pang of disappointment and longing followed after him, but I stubbornly reminded myself that he was trying to teach me archery in order to defend myself against the creepy crawlies of the Otherworld. An image of the little gnomes that had chased after me a handful of months ago and the memory of my near-death experience on the swinging bridge forced my focus back onto the task at hand.

"When I say so, release the bowstring."

Cade gave me the signal and I let loose the string. It slapped against the leather of my other glove and the arrow went sailing, though not nearly as far as his own.

I slumped my shoulders in disappointment. How pathetic I must look to him.

"Good!" Cade called from behind me.

I turned around and looked at him, my eyebrows raised. "Really?"

He smiled again, curse him. "Your arrow flew forward, didn't it?"

For a while I felt that tingle of self-consciousness again, but when I gave him a closer look, I realized he was teasing me.

I gasped in mock outrage and crossed my arms. He only laughed.

"We'll just stick to archery today. Later, we'll get into hand to hand combat. But if you can take your enemy out with an arrow, that would be best. Some of the creatures of the Otherworld have poisonous skin and horns that could really hurt you if they get a hold of you."

I shivered at the thought of those little gnomes or that red demon-squirrel clinging to my legs or wrapping their arms around me. I was pretty sure they wouldn't be as gentle or smell as good as Cade.

We spent the remains of the morning plunking arrows into the target. Cade played the role of the perfect instructor, never being too hard on me and never trying to sugar-coat my ego. We kept our conversation strictly business: only questions about archery and defense against Otherworldly creatures. I wanted so badly to ask him normal every day questions, like who his parents were, if he ever went to school in the Otherworld, what kind of music he liked. If he had a girlfriend . . .

I bit my lip and got back to aiming an arrow. I told myself that this was not the time to ask such questions, but if I was being honest, it was only because I was afraid to ask him. He might think I was nosy or give me answers I didn't want to hear.

Cade walked me home after our practice, well, he walked me to the oak tree we used as our own personal mail box, but in my mind it was as good as walking me home. He stopped and leaned against the tree and I turned to face him. He looked pensive, as if his mind was a world away. I laughed inwardly. It probably was a world away, or an *Other*world away.

I cleared my throat and decided to break the awkward silence. "I appreciate all you are doing for me, really I do. But I still have a lot of questions, you know."

He nodded, but didn't move from where he stood. The bows, both unstrung, he had leaned against the tree and the quivers with them.

"I can't answer all of your questions Meghan, but I will answer those that I'm permitted to."

I thought that was weird. "What do you mean those that you are permitted to?"

He winced, so insignificantly that I almost didn't see it, and then let out a worrisome sigh. He met my eyes, his own dark green and shifting towards brown. "It's complicated," he said.

Oh, like I hadn't heard *that* excuse before. I crossed my arms and arched my brow. His grin didn't help in my determination to look domineering.

He pushed away from the tree and stepped forward, stopping a foot away from me and forcing me to crane my neck back to see his face. I couldn't imagine anyone not permitting him to do anything.

"Okay, fine, what about the raven then. It tried to push me over the edge of a bridge. I know it is Otherworldly because it has been following me."

Cade blanched and took a step back. I took that as a bad sign.

"You are correct in surmising the raven is Otherworldly. It is an enemy and you need to avoid it at all costs."

I didn't like the sound of that. "Why? Why is it trying to kill me?"

Cade shrugged and actually looked guilty. "I don't know yet. All that I know is that it plans on trying again."

Before I could demand that he tell me how he knew all this, I heard Bradley's voice call out from our backyard somewhere.

"Meghan! Is that you down there?"

Cursing, I turned to see if my annoying brothers had been spying. Apparently Bradley had only heard my voice. I turned to address Cade one last time, but he was already ducking behind the oak tree. He had grabbed his bow and quiver, but not mine. I arched a brow at him.

"Keep them Meghan. In case you need them."

And then he and Fergus slipped into the woods the way a garter snake disappears into a field of tall grass.

Smitten

I gazed at the bow and quiver. Where on earth was I going to store these where my parents and brothers wouldn't find them? I decided to hide them behind the tree for now. I would clean out a spot in the back of my closet where no one, me included, ever went. If I were to take them up right now, my brothers would see them for sure and the questions would never cease.

Sighing, I trudged up the hill and called out ahead of me so Bradley would hear, "Yeah, just got back."

I still had plenty of questions that hadn't been answered, and I was slightly annoyed that I had let Cade charm me out of my common sense, but what was done was done. I would just have to be careful not to let myself get so beguiled next time. *Just don't look into his eyes Meghan; don't look at his mouth when he smiles. Focus on something else.*

But I knew now more than ever that there wasn't a single place on Cade MacRoich that wouldn't leave me gaping like a groupie at my first concert. Perhaps it was that Otherworld glamour he had mentioned that made him so irresistible. Or maybe I was just a complete and utter fool.

Fifteen

Confession

The New Year passed and along with it the remains of the winter season. I didn't see Cade for weeks after our break, but I had the memory of spending time with him in the swamp to keep me warm during those cold days. I had hidden the bow and arrows in the back of my closet, just as I had planned, then got back to my routine of checking the oak tree on a daily basis. Okay, maybe more like an hourly basis. Three days after our practice, I found two old, leather-bound books at the base of the tree with a note attached to them.

Meghan,

Here are some Celtic legends that get as close to the truth as possible. The rest you will have to learn over time and perhaps one day when you are ready to come to the Otherworld, you will finally know everything.

C.M.

Of course, the gift made me giddy and I immediately dove into the books. The first one was a saga about a great battle between the native beings of Ireland, the Fomorians, and another group that arrived later, the Tuatha De Danann. The writing was archaic and dry, but I forced myself to finish it, making note of the characters and their roles.

The second book Cade had left me was a little more interesting (about a war started over a cow of all things). I think this one stuck with me more because it featured Cuchulainn, the hero on the cover of the Irish Myths book I had picked up on the shopping spree with Tully and Robyn. In that story, Cuchulainn was called upon to fight an entire army. During a few of his exploits he even came face to face with the Morrigan.

It was late when I finally got tired of flipping through the books. They hadn't answered all of my questions, well, at least not the ones I wanted answers to, but they had given me a better taste of what I might be dealing with. I was starting to seriously reconsider the idea that the raven stalking me might be a minion of the Morrigan's. I had dismissed it at first because I didn't think I was important enough for a goddess to bother with. But now that I thought about it, maybe I was. After all, I didn't even know who I was, at least not in Otherworldly terms. Cade had only told me I was Faelorehn, a being from the Otherworld and he himself admitted that he didn't know everything about me.

I sighed and flipped my pillow over, seeking the cool side. It was hard to sleep when I was trying to solve a great mystery and I didn't even have all the clues. I would simply just have to wait for Cade to return and demand answers this time. No more letting him distract me with his good looks and archery skills. It was time he started explaining a few things, and I didn't care how 'complicated' it was. There were some things I just needed to know (like why I was a target to begin with) before some demented Otherworldly faelah got the better of me.

I was left to my own devices for the next couple of weeks, and luckily I had school to distract me once again. Also, to my great relief, I didn't see a single faelah creature that entire time. Of course, it meant I didn't see Cade either. I grew restless and I was beginning to brush my friends aside whenever they'd invite me over.

Halfway through that second week, it dawned upon me that maybe I was growing obsessed with a guy that was darting in and out of my life like some self-propelled yo-yo. It wasn't healthy.

Gritting my teeth and taking on a newly found determination, I told myself to forget about Cade MacRoich and to start living my life again. Who knew when he'd decide to visit this world again? Maybe I was Faelorehn, but I had been around humans long enough to know I enjoyed hanging out with my friends.

When Tully asked me if I wanted to come over that weekend for a movie with Robyn and the guys, I smiled and agreed without a second thought. The movie helped distract me, but it didn't erase everything I'd learned in the past few months. And if I was being completely honest with myself, I didn't want to forget everything, especially not Cade.

I sighed and eyed my clock, secretly wishing that my reflective thoughts would go away. It was almost midnight on a Sunday and I had school in the morning. But I couldn't sleep. I had tried doing some more Otherworld research earlier, but the websites just kept repeating the same old information over and over again. I read a few of the folk legends from my Irish Myths book, but when I started reading a story about Cuchulainn, I threw the book down on my desk and climbed into bed. The Irish hero reminded me too much of Cade.

I sighed heavily and felt the tears forming in my eyes. Who was I kidding? I missed Cade. I missed him terribly, and it was high time I stop lying to myself. Yes, I knew hardly anything about him and yes he was never around. But during those few hours we'd spent together, he hadn't belittled or avoided me. He hadn't glanced away in disgust. I know it seems silly, but I just knew that Cade MacRoich understood me; had seen me for who I was, and I was finally willing to admit that I had fallen for him. Hard.

◉ ◉ ◉

One day after school, an entire month and a half since I'd last seen Cade, I decided to decline Thomas's offer for a ride home and I took the back way through the swamp. I wasn't worried about getting ambushed by Adam Peders or Michaela West; they hadn't bothered me since Cade had threatened Adam. A twinge of regret coursed through me, but I shook it off. *He may never come back again Meg. Time to get over this infatuation.* Of course, walking through the very woods where I had first met him wasn't the brightest idea. Oh well.

I should've been worried about running into faelah in the woods, but the truth of the matter was, I didn't care. I was tired of being afraid; tired of waiting for someone to give me answers. Huffing a deep breath, I hiked my backpack further up onto my shoulders and began the gentle climb up the equestrian trail. I kept my head down, allowing a stray curl to obscure my vision. It wasn't until I reached the old oak tree that I noticed the wolfhound. In fact, he had to yip at me before I passed him up. That only startled me into a small scream.

"Fergus!" I hissed, willing my heartbeat to slow.

The great white hound whined and gestured towards the tree. I had told myself I didn't care if Cade ever showed himself again. That was a lie. I could tell by the way my stomach fluttered and my knees grew wobbly. And all this at the prospect of getting a note from him.

I dropped my backpack and reached up into the tree, my fingers fumbling around for the knothole. My fingertips brushed parchment and I grabbed it, yanking a note free of its hiding place.

Quickly, I dropped back to the ground and broke the seal, not caring if I ruined it this time. My eyes darted across the page, and my heart felt like it was melting.

Meghan,

I beg your forgiveness for staying away so long, but things have been unstable here in the Otherworld. I will be arriving in your world soon. I wish to discuss something of an important matter with you. I hope you have been well, and I hope to see you again soon.

C.M.

I read the date and time he indicated on the note. Friday afternoon. Tomorrow. My heart leapt into my throat. I blinked up at Fergus, but he merely panted, his rusty colored ears perked backwards. How on earth was I going to get any sleep tonight?

⊚ ⊚ ⊚

Just as I'd predicted, I was tired the next morning from a night spent tossing and turning and daydreaming about Cade. I continued to struggle through my classes the next day, trying to stay focused, but all I could think about was a pair of changeable, green Faelorehn eyes and the confident smile that went with them. Finally, the bell announcing the end of class rang and I made a bee line for the field behind school.

Although Cade wasn't due for another hour or so, I went straight to the clearing in the swamp. Thomas had invited us over to hang out with him during his sister's Quinceañera and normally I would have gone, but I told him I already had plans. Everyone had eyed me suspiciously as if they thought I was lying. For once, I wasn't.

As I waited, I pulled at the bark from the old fallen eucalyptus I leaned against. My nerves were frazzled and my skin felt clammy. *Knock it off Meg!* I told myself. *He's just a guy!* If only.

Finally, the crack of brush sounded behind me and I whipped around. Trotting down the path that led deeper into the swamp was Fergus, followed by Cade. My heart stopped working for a few moments as I watched his tall, confident frame come into view. But something was wrong. He looked hunched over and as he moved closer, he seemed to stagger as he walked. Concern soon replaced my feeling of anticipation.

He chose to walk around the log instead of jumping over it, and came to stand several feet in front of me.

"Meghan," he breathed, his face breaking into a wide smile.

On any normal day, I would have melted into a puddle at his feet, for he sounded as if the sight of me standing there was the greatest thing in the world to him. But his appearance took the joy right out of the moment. He looked absolutely haggard; how I would have expected him to look had he truly been a homeless man and not simply pretending to be one. His hair, usually tousled but well cared for, looked greasy and unkempt. His eyes seemed empty and their color was so close to black I couldn't tell his pupils from his irises. Deep shadows painted the space beneath his eyes and his skin looked as pallid as death.

"Cade," I said, my voice pitched low, "what has happened to you?"

He winced, and even that small action looked painful. Fergus whined softly next to him.

Cade ran his fingers through his hair, that familiar action I had come to recognize as a sign of distress. I stood there, leaning against the fallen tree, not knowing what to do. I crossed my arms and watched him, waiting for some signal to either hug him or stay put. Hugging him would be ideal, but I wasn't brave enough to offer up that form of comfort. He glanced at the ground, took a breath as if to speak, then ran his hands through his hair again.

"What's wrong?" I asked again, trying to keep the quiver from my voice.

Something was clearly agitating him and I had a feeling that it had something to do with me. Hadn't his note said so? And if Cade, the Otherworldly bounty hunter/assassin extraordinaire was nervous, then I was nervous cubed, maybe even to the fourth or fifth power.

Finally he stopped running his hands through his hair and instead placed them on his hips, slouching a little. He wasn't facing me, but he turned his head to the side and finally gave me his full attention. I nearly fell over. His eyes were so haunted, and he looked even more run down than I had thought on first examination. What in the world, or more appropriately, what in the Otherworld had done this to him?

I pushed away from the log and slowly reached out my hand. Just as quickly I snatched it back to my side. What was I thinking? A fleeting image of me walking up to him and placing my hand gently on his face to comfort him flashed in my mind, followed by a similar image of him taking me in his arms to help soothe his troubled thoughts. Ridiculous. I might have a major crush on him, but that didn't mean he returned those feelings.

He sighed and looked away again, his impressive height and bulk seeming to diminish.

"I discovered some troubling information, that's all."

That's all? Troubling information? What did that mean and how could he refer to it so nonchalantly if he was behaving this way because of it?

"What kind of information?"

He nodded. "About you."

That shook me. I knew he had wanted to discuss something of importance with me, but I had no idea it would be construed as troubling. I gaped at him, suddenly feeling light-headed.

"Wh-what do you mean? Troubling? How is it troubling? Is someone else after me? Are there more faelah looking for me?" I babbled.

Cade stepped closer, reaching out a hand, and for a split-second I thought he might actually act on that fantasy I'd envisioned earlier. But he stopped short and pulled his hand into a fist, letting it drop to his side. He bowed his head and took a deep breath.

"What I learned is that you may be the daughter of a Tuatha De Danann and a Fomorian."

I blinked. Huh? Why was that troubling exactly? I recalled the story of the great battle between the Tuatha De and the Fomorians and how most of the Celtic pantheon was associated with the Tuatha De. I knew, according to my internet searches and from the books Cade had given me, that there were a few Faelorehn descended from both lines and that they were often responsible for mischief, but really, I had no designs on upturning the Otherworld. Me? Wreaking havoc in a world of magical monsters and powerful gods? I almost nearly choked on a laugh.

Confession

I couldn't even stand up to the school bullies and their only weapons were harsh words.

"I never discussed the Tuatha De Danann or the Fomorians with you," Cade said, almost apologetically.

I held up a hand. "The Fomorians are the magical natives of Ireland and the more demon-like of the two and the Tuatha De arrived during one of the invasions of Ireland. Most of the Celtic gods and goddesses are associated with the Tuatha De."

Cade actually smiled. "You have been doing your research, haven't you?"

That warmed me, despite the lingering chill of Cade's news.

"I don't understand," I finally said. "Why is that troubling? Isn't everyone in the Otherworld, well besides the faelah of course, either Fomorian or Tuatha De? And aren't some of them both?"

I was very confused, and terrified. Not necessarily because of this news, but because of the way Cade looked at me then, as if I were one of the grotesque little gnomes that had chased after me several months ago.

"It's troubling because when a Faelorehn child is born to one Tuatha De parent and one Fomorian parent, often times they come with at least one major character flaw that will surely lead into ruin."

Basically, he was telling me I was a ticking time bomb. My shoulders drooped and I fought the urge to cry. A cadre of thoughts buzzed through my head: *he said you may be a descendent of a Fomorian and a Tuatha De Meg, you* may *be, nothing definite . . . and it's the twenty-first century for goodness' sake! People don't behave like barbarians anymore! Who knows, maybe your character flaw is the inability to act like a normal, socially obsessed, mall visiting, cell phone texting teen. Chin up!*

But of course, my mind decided to dwell on the one, single worst thought it could conjure: *of course you have a flaw, duh! This is why you were abandoned to begin with!*

I shook my head and cleared my throat. No need to panic. Yet. I looked up at Cade, hoping those weren't tears I felt swimming in my eyes.

"What do you mean by character flaw?" Annoying conscience or not, I wanted to know all the details.

Cade shifted his weight and crossed his arms. The late afternoon light only made his gaunt features more pronounced. I frowned in sympathy. What would he do if I tried to comfort him? Probably break my neck in one swift movement. I was flawed, remember? Just because he helped me before didn't mean he wanted to now. Not after learning I was half god, half demon.

"Do you remember the story of Bres?"

I narrowed my eyes and tilted my head, trying to recall. After a few seconds I nodded. "Led the Fomorians against the Tuatha De in the great battle of Maige Tuired." I had read it in one of the books he had given me.

Cade nodded. "His mother was Fomorian; his father Tuatha De. He made the mistake of claiming sovereignty through his mother's line, unbalanced the Celtic social structure, and therefore brought about war and mayhem. That is how the story goes, at least from the Celts' perspective. In truth, Bres's mixed blood gave him more power than most Faelorehn and he used it to drive a wedge between the two races of Eilé. His flaw was arrogance, something that was only fed by his power."

I licked my lips. I could see how being arrogant and powerful could ruin a king and his kingdom. Had it not happened in earth's own history? But what sort of flaw could I possibly have that would lead to war? I almost snorted. Well, I knew for sure it wasn't arrogance.

"So, you're saying I'm going to somehow wreak havoc in the Otherworld because of a flaw I have?" How could I do that when I wasn't even *in* the Otherworld?

Cade didn't speak.

Confession

I sighed. My initial fear had ebbed but I was still a bit jumpy. I told myself that just because I was half Fomorian and half Tuatha De didn't mean I had to follow in Bres's footsteps. Perhaps we could prevent any major catastrophes if I knew what to expect.

"Well, what is my character flaw then?" I asked, crossing my arms in an attempt to stop the nervous fluttering in my stomach.

Cade looked up. At least his eyes were looking less black and more jade now. "I don't know. You may already be displaying it, or it may be lying dormant, waiting for you to awaken it in the Otherworld."

Cade drew another long breath, letting it out slowly. "I know I said you weren't ready to visit the Otherworld, but I think you should know how to get there, just in case."

Wait, he was telling me my character flaw might come suddenly to life if I crossed over to the Otherworld and now he wanted to show me how to get there?

I must have had a look of bafflement on my face, because he snorted and said, "I know it seems even more dangerous now, knowing that you could very well have the potential to cause chaos in Eile. But the future seems uncertain from where I stand and I'm willing to take the risk."

What was he saying?

"If something happens here and I'm not around to help you, I want you to have another option."

Cade looked troubled; sad even. I felt another spark of fear course through me. Before I could say anything, he gestured for me to follow him back down the trail from where he had come. I went wordlessly, with Fergus trailing behind us.

Cade spoke as we walked, the quiet woods standing witness to our progress.

"I would rather take you to the Otherworld myself, but current circumstances forbid me from doing so. You would be helpless until you grew into your power, but that takes time. Yet I fear that if you remain here, should certain events come to pass, you would be more exposed to danger than if you were in the Otherworld. Until we know how your mixed blood is going to affect Eilé, it is best to keep you safe and hidden. Some people would rather see you dead than risk learning whether or not you are a threat."

Cade stopped and turned to look at me. He placed his hands on my shoulders and caught my gaze. I shivered.

"I have told others about you, other Faelorehn whom I trust. They know to help you if you arrive in the Otherworld alone."

"But," I whispered harshly, my jumbled thoughts barely breaking through my shell-shocked mind, "why are you even helping me if I'm such a danger to the Otherworld?"

Cade sighed, one thumb lifting off my shoulder to gently graze my neck. It was through sheer willpower alone that I didn't fall against him. He looked off to the side, then squared his jaw and glanced back at me, his eyes flashing between green and black. "Not every Tuatha De-Fomorian Faelorehn brings harm upon Eilé. It is when they are found by the wrong people and exploited that causes problems. If your power or flaw is strong Meghan, then you would make a very useful weapon to the wrong people. I'm hoping that we can avoid those people, but I might be too late."

His thumb stopped its caress but it stayed pressed against my neck. My mind and senses were on overdrive, but eventually coherent thoughts started bubbling to the surface. Why was Cade telling me this? What did he mean, if I arrived alone in the Otherworld and he might be too late? Why wouldn't he be the one to take me? Then it dawned upon me. His exhaustion, his haunted eyes, this little speech, the way he had brushed his thumb over my skin as if trying to comfort me . . . He was expecting someone to do harm to me, and not just a raven trying to knock me off a bridge or a pack of gnomes trying to scratch at my legs. He was expecting someone to bring down a war upon me or to take me and turn me into a monster, and he was planning to defend me. Defend me but not survive.

I must have cried out and lost my balance, because Cade's arm was now under my elbow, supporting my weight.

No. I wanted to scream. *No!* I didn't want some demented army of faelah to kill me, and I didn't want Cade to die either. I started to cry for real this time.

"No Meghan, you must know how to get to the Otherworld."

He grabbed my arm, a little more roughly than usual, and practically dragged me along. We came to the end of the path and turned right, down a great gully carved from years of rain. The sand was smooth beneath my feet and our path was blocked by eucalyptus trees that had fallen victim to the eroded hillside.

Finally we came to the end of the culvert and Cade stopped. My arm would be bruised, but I didn't care. I was too upset; upset at too many things. I had just learned my true identity a handful of months ago and now I would be fighting for my life without the proper tools I needed. It was so unbearably unfair.

"Meghan," Cade said gently, gesturing towards a place in the canyon wall where several fallen trees had accumulated.

A dark hole in the side of the earth sat behind it, half hidden by strips of hanging bark and branches. A chill covered my body when I saw the cave and I quailed away from it.

"Although it is covered by the hillside," Cade was saying quietly as he stared at the black maw, "there is a dolmarehn there. If you enter this cave, it will take you to the Otherworld. But Meghan," he turned me towards him and grabbed my arms once more, gently this time. His voice was harsh when he spoke again, "you must promise me you will not enter the Otherworld unless you feel you have no other choice."

I nodded numbly.

"Promise me!" he hissed as he shook me.

"I, I promise," I whispered as a tear streaked down my cheek.

Just then, a stale, cold breeze poured from the cave, followed by the sound of distant murmuring. I thought my bones had frozen.

Cade stiffened. "I must go," he said with no emotion.

Before he stepped past the fallen trees and into the cavern, he reached back and touched my cheek, wiping away my stray tears. He smiled, even though his green eyes held sadness, then disappeared into the dark. Fergus, who had remained strangely quiet this entire time, whined and followed after him.

I was left standing in complete disbelief, staring blankly into a hole in the ground that I was sure was haunted. My mind was far too overwhelmed to think clearly, but a few things surfaced in my mind before I forced myself to walk home. I was in danger, more so than I thought. If I really was some Fomorian, Tuatha De hybrid, and if I really could be a potential threat, then it wasn't too far-fetched to believe those of the Otherworld would want me eliminated. Or worse, would want to use me in order to destroy their enemies. If that raven that had been following me really was a pet of the Morrigan, then she could very well be the one after me. Yes, I was in trouble, but so was Cade. Although he never actually said the words, he had indicated that he would fight to defend me and he didn't expect to survive such a battle.

A sob left my chest, and I clutched my arms around my waist. I had to get away from this portal, this cave to the Otherworld, before I was tempted enough to run after him.

I arrived home to find the house empty. Good. I couldn't face my family now, not after everything I had just learned. I got undressed, took a long, hot shower, and then got into bed. I was immensely glad that tomorrow was Saturday because there was no way I could face my friends in the morning. I would need the weekend to recover and decide what I was going to do next. No, I would not sit back and just let some Otherworldly thing kill or kidnap me, but according to Cade, the odds definitely were not in my favor.

Sixteen

Depressed

Naturally, I was depressed all that week. Tully and Robyn asked me constantly what was wrong, but I merely shrugged and mumbled some lame excuse. They told me that I'd been acting strange for weeks and insisted I tell them what was bothering me.

"Is it some guy?" Robyn asked as she sucked the last of her soda through a neon bendy straw.

I drew in a breath then shook my head. *Well, yes and no,* I thought to myself. I couldn't tell them everything I knew even if I wanted to. I wasn't the only one involved at that point and even if I was, they would finally see me as everyone else did: a freak.

Okay guys, do you really want to hear the truth? I'm not human after all. Nope, I'm Faelorehn, from the Otherworld. Immortal. Remember that huge raven that tried to kill me? Yeah, it was from the Otherworld too, and apparently I'm some freakish, demon-god half-breed that may or may not inadvertently destroy the structure of the Otherworld, so you might want to keep your distance in case any other rogue faelah are after me. Oh, and you were right about the guy. He's the one who told me all of this, but it doesn't matter, because he is perfect and has the most amazing eyes and he might die any day now trying to keep all these Otherworldly creepy crawlers away from me.

I didn't say it out loud of course. No, I didn't have the guts to, and Tully and Robyn wouldn't believe me anyway. But thinking about Cade made me suddenly miserable and embarrassed at the same time. He must think I'm a huge threat and a complete waste of time. My cheeks started to warm as I recalled how foolish I had acted around him.

Robyn smacked me in the back and laughed, "I knew it!"

"Robyn!" Tully growled, "Can't you see she's depressed?"

I blinked up at them, confused. My internal tirade had sapped my attention for the last minute or two. Then I remembered what Robyn had asked me before and my blush deepened. They wanted to know about Cade.

"Oh, sorry," Robyn said. She crumpled her can and chucked it into the nearest recycling bin. "Wanna talk about it?"

I gave her a glare and shook my head. That was Robyn's way of saying, 'Please give me the details!'

"Oh, come on, it will make you feel better," she insisted, patting me this time instead of smacking me.

"No, really, it isn't what you think," I blurted. Liar. It was exactly what she thought. Sort of. I was miserable because I liked a boy and he didn't like me back. Ugh, that was a lie too. If only it were that simple.

"Is it someone who goes to school here?" Robyn grimaced as she said it, knowing how we both felt about the boys at our high school.

"Robyn, she doesn't want to talk. Remember what happened the last time we bugged her about one of her crushes?"

Despite my focus on the downward spiral my life had become, I cringed at the memory. It had been in junior high and the boy of my dreams had been inconveniently walking by when I blurted his name out as my secret crush to my pestering friends. I tried to fake illness for the rest of the week, but Mom would have nothing of it. The weeks that followed had been some of the worst of my life. I had a bad feeling that one of these days I would end up looking back and laughing at how insignificant they were, but I had an even nastier feeling that worse situations loomed ahead. The bell announcing the end of lunch rang and I was brought back to the present.

"Oh, fine!" Robyn complained. "But you're going to have to spill the beans eventually. Oh! Maybe at our Beltaine festival in a few weeks! It will be the perfect time to divulge anything to do with romance." She winked and skipped off in the direction of her next class.

"Beltaine?" Tully asked, looking confused.

"May first. It's a Celtic festival that celebrates the beginning of the light half of the year, or the start of spring," I said.

Tully stopped and looked at me in surprise. "How do you know that?"

I paused outside the door to our math class. I had forgotten that, for the past several months, I had kept my research of the Celtic world a secret from my friends. Because, let's face it, they would wonder at my sudden interest in the myths and legends of the ancient people of Ireland. I cursed myself. How could I be so careless? Oh yeah, duh. Gloom and doom headed my way soon, *and* the stupid side effects that resulted from pining after a guy.

"Um, well, Robyn went off on a tangent the other day after she dropped you off after school."

I smiled, but the look Tully gave me told me she wasn't convinced. The tardy bell rang and as Mr. Skaring glared at us as we took our seats, I was grateful. It meant Tully couldn't question me further and I was certain that the oh-so fascinating world of pre-calculus would bludgeon any memories of the past hour out of her mind.

I didn't see Cade for the rest of the week or for the rest of the next week either. I was partly relieved, for the distance from him gave me time to sort through my turbulent feelings. He had said he only thought I *might* be half Fomorian and half Tuatha De. Maybe he had been wrong and maybe this whole thing was a huge misunderstanding and an overreaction on his part and on mine as well. Perhaps he had figured out his error and was now talking with the Faelorehn being who kept sending ravens and demons after me.

Even if all that were true and I didn't have to worry about the threat of impending death, that didn't help with the way I felt about Cade. I tried, for the umpteenth time, to convince myself that it was just a silly crush I had on him and that it would soon pass. He was too old for me anyway, and I'd be going off to college in a year. Then I remembered that I probably *wouldn't* be going off to college, since I wasn't human, and that I would most likely be going to the Otherworld instead. That is, if I could prove I really wasn't a threat to their society. That got the emotional rollercoaster going all over again.

Robyn's Beltaine party didn't help matters. She decided, since her family was extremely religious, and since she really didn't have a backyard and the swamp behind my house wouldn't do (thank goodness; it held too many memories for me at the moment), that our little pagan celebration was to take place at a local park in town. We each had to bring a selection of flowers, 'plucked from a wild field or growing naturally in our yard'. I think the ones I brought were technically weeds. After the initial prayers and thanks she gave to the gods and goddesses (all names I now recognized), we sat around in a circle and recited some sort of chant. When parents started dragging their curious children away, muttering something about 'freaks' and 'rotten teenagers', I knew the festivities had just begun. Well, at least the weather was finally nice again.

When Michaela, Veronica and half the cheerleading squad arrived to practice, I wondered if I could conjure up flying pinecones again. Of course, there wasn't a single pinecone in sight. Luckily, the strange droning of our voices blocked out most of the horrible girls' shrill laughter and crude remarks. After a while they got bored and moved on to a different part of the park to commence with their practice.

Depressed

The one good thing that did come out of visiting the park was that, once we were through with the 'ceremony', we left the grassy lawn behind and climbed down into the area where the creek was located. The trees provided ample shade and for some reason or another, my nerves felt more at peace there. Perhaps it was the presence of the soothing stream, or the quiet of the shady trees. Will and Thomas wandered off to explore the creek while Robyn, Tully and I picked a low hanging sycamore limb to relax on.

"So, spill," Robyn said as she tossed the remains of her flower garland into the lazy water below.

I blinked at her, not knowing what she was talking about.

"The boy you've been mooning over! I know he doesn't go to our school, because, let's face it, all the boys there are cretins. And I've been watching you for the past two weeks. You haven't been making eyes at anyone. So it must be an outsider."

"Robyn! Thomas and Will are cretins?" Tully scoffed, folding her arms across her chest.

Robyn snorted, picking a leaf off of her old tattered jeans. "No, but Meghan isn't pining after one of them." She gave me a quick glance. "Or are you?"

I thrust my arms down against the tree trunk, nearly falling off. "No! Thomas and Will are like my cousins."

"Then who is it? Have we seen him before?"

I sighed. She would never let this go until I provided her with some information. I really didn't want to think about Cade for the time being, but perhaps I could twist the truth just enough to get Robyn off my back. Besides, it's not like they'd believe me if I told them the truth . . .

"Ugh, fine!" I hissed. "His name's C-Clay."

Uh, Clay? That was the best name I could come up with? I gave a mental groan.

"Oh, do go on. What does he look like? Where did you meet him?"

Faeloren

To my utter disbelief (and relief) Robyn, and Tully even, bought it.

I proceeded to tell them everything about 'Clay', his blond hair and brown eyes, how shy he was and how I was taller than him. The exact opposite of Cade. Paranoid person that I was, I didn't want to risk my friends catching a glimpse of Cade and recognizing him as Clay. That would be disastrous on so many levels. So far I had managed to keep all of the chaos of my Otherworldly self separate from my normal, human self. Okay, maybe not so normal, but still. Whatever being Otherworldly meant for me in the long run, I didn't want my friends mixed up in it, especially after Cade's insinuation that I could be leading a very dangerous existence.

" . . . well, I think most boys our age are shorter than you, Meg. Don't listen to Robyn."

I caught the tail end of what Tully had been saying, but it didn't matter. They had believed my ridiculous story and now that their curiosity was satisfied, they might actually leave me alone for a while.

We stayed in the park until sunset, and then we all piled into Thomas's minivan and headed back home. Tully and I were the last ones dropped off and as we waved goodbye to Thomas, I caught a glimpse of something lurking in the bushes. My stomach clenched and I looked over at Tully. She hadn't seen it. Of course not. Was it happening already? The threat Cade had warned me about? Was an army of faelah going to pour out of the trees at any second and tear me to shreds right there in the middle of the street? I was suddenly petrified, but I couldn't let anything happen to Tully. She was my best friend. I had to be the brave one.

"Well, I had better get home," I said through a nervous cough. "Still have homework to finish."

I darted my eyes towards the bushes again, but the thing was gone. It didn't make me feel any easier though.

Depressed

"K, bye," Tully said. As she walked up to her front door, she looked back at me once more. "I hope things work out with you and Clay," she said with a smile. "Maybe we should all go to a movie or something?"

I was too distracted by my sudden fear, so I didn't quite hear her. "Sure, maybe. We'll see," I babbled as I waved goodbye.

I started up the street at a fast pace and kept my eye on the landscape behind me. Ugh, if only we hadn't stayed out so late. Twilight was creeping in and the grey shadows of the trees provided lots of hiding places for anything with malicious intent.

I was sure Tully gave me one of her looks before disappearing inside her house, but I was too distracted to notice. Once I was sure she was safely inside, I started running. I moved as fast as possible, my ears prickling to catch the sound of pursuit. I was three doors down from my own house when I heard the loud padding of feet and the panting of a large animal just behind me. My heart rate went up, making it hard to breathe and move my legs. And then, for some strange reason, I looked behind me. Hadn't I always been the one, while watching horror movies with my friends, who screamed at the main character not to slow down or look behind them? Hadn't I told them how stupid they were, that if they had just kept going they would have made it inside the house in time to lock out the machete-wielding villain?

Well, turns out I was well ahead of my pursuer. I would have made it, except the shock of seeing it turned my legs to jelly. It wasn't one of the Cúmorrig, nor was it a pack of those demonic gnomes or that vile squirrel I had seen chatting with the raven. This thing was far bigger, about the size of a bull, but it looked like some horrible mutation of a human and a goat.

It walked upright and its eyes were huge and milky white. Rotting teeth that came to a point filled its mouth. Thick mats of black and gray fur hung from its neck and head. Its torso was that of a man, but from the waist down it looked like some monstrous, skinny goat, cloven hooves and all. Three long, spiraled horns protruded from its head and when it screamed, a fetid smell filled the air. I couldn't keep a sob of fear from escaping my mouth.

It snarled at me, snapping as it approached slowly, its pitch-black hooves clacking against the ground as if they were made of iron. I couldn't move; I was frozen in fear. It lurched towards me and I ducked to the ground, covering my head. I was certain that at some point I screamed.

Nothing happened, but I could hear the creature growling in anger. I risked a glance. It was pacing again, and then it lunged for a third time, faster than anything I had ever seen. I didn't have time to cover my head this time, but before my brain could force my lungs to produce another scream, the animal sidled back. I was dumbfounded and confused. It tried to get at me once again and was once again thwarted. It was as if some invisible force field had established itself around my body. The nightmarish animal was angry, but no matter how hard it tried to tear at me with its claws, it couldn't get to me.

I was so wrapped up in my own terror and fascination that I didn't at first hear the barking. I saw Fergus before I really heard him, leaping like a white blur onto the fetid, black haired back of my attacker. My relief hit me like a tidal wave. The demonic creature screamed in pain and anger, and before I knew it, Fergus was chasing it back into the trees that led down into the swamp. I hoped he nipped its heels all the way back to where it had come from. Some hellish part of the Otherworld, probably.

"Meghan? Meghan! Goodness girl, are you alright?"

I blinked up to find my neighbor, Mrs. Dollard, hovering over me, her gardening sheers hanging loose in her gloved hands. I choked back a sob. Dear lord, did she see that thing? She was such a kind old woman, I hoped with all my heart that Fergus had chased it off before she rushed out here to see what all the commotion was about.

She blinked at me over her thick glasses. She looked utterly confused, but although she was well over seventy she was renowned for her sharp mind. It wasn't like she would have been oblivious to what had just happened. Then it hit me. Of course she didn't see what had happened. She was human and these horrible apparitions were only revealing themselves to me.

"Uhm," I looked at her skirt, grass stains where the knees should be. "Bee," I blurted.

She made an effort to stand up straight and push her glasses back onto her nose. She pursed her wrinkled lips and adjusted herself so that she stood, elbows akimbo, and glared down at me.

"Well, of all the silly nonsense. Really girl, a bee? You do know they are extremely beneficial insects, pollinating our flowers for us and making honey . . ." she mumbled as she shuffled her way back to her house.

I cringed. I liked bees, really I did, but how else could I have explained my strange behavior? Had she seen me running and then diving for the ground? Screaming as I covered my head? Maybe not. It was getting dark after all.

Reluctantly, I stood up and brushed the gravel from my jeans. The heels of my hands were scraped, but not too badly. I cast a nervous glance down the road, towards my house and in the direction of where that nightmare had disappeared to. Was it still out there? Would it come back? Was Fergus alright? Had Cade come with him?

Before thinking much longer about it, I began to walk briskly towards home. Once there, I waved a quick hello to my mother and brothers, mumbled something about laundry and homework, and went down to my room. I double checked to make sure my sliding glass door was locked, recovered the mistletoe charm Cade had given me months before from among the necklaces hanging from my bed post, and curled up in bed with a pen and some paper.

Cade,

I lifted my pen and thought about what I should say. I knew he was preoccupied; busy with whatever he was busy with in the

Otherworld. But it couldn't hurt to try. Eventually, I got back to work.

Cade,

I know it has been a long time since I've seen you, and I know you are concerned about my heritage and what trouble it might cause, but I need to talk with you. I was attacked by something Otherworldly today. Not the raven or the Cúmorrig or even the gnomes, but something much worse.

I thought about describing it and telling him about its strange behavior (how it couldn't really attack me) but my hand was shaking too much and I needed to write something that would entice him to come and see me.

Please send Fergus to my door when you are ready to meet. I would feel safer if he were there to escort me.

Sincerely,

Meghan

Okay, that wasn't all that enticing, but perhaps he would come anyway. I glanced out my door, debating whether or not I should place the note in the knothole tonight. When a flash of crimson eyes glared back at me through the growing dusk from the trees in the distance, I quickly checked the lock on my door one more time and drew the blinds.

My heart pounding in my throat, I dug through my closet, tossing my empty suitcase and several boxes of old photographs out of the way. When all of the clutter was cleared out, I scooped up the bow and quiver of arrows Cade had given to me. I didn't care if my mom or my brothers stumbled upon it in the night. There was no way I was going to sleep without some form of protection within reach. And honestly, I didn't think I was going to sleep at all.

Seventeen

Betrayed

ust as I had predicted, I spent the night tossing and turning, waiting for that grotesque goat-man to break through my sliding glass door and maul me in my sleep. When my alarm went off at six, I merely groaned and got up. I really didn't feel like going to school, but I knew it would be safer than staying at home all day, waiting for that monster to make its move. I figured being surrounded by hundreds of other students would work in my favor.

The one good thing that came out of my terrifying ordeal from the day before was that I wasn't thinking too much about Cade. Well, at least I *hadn't* been thinking too much about Cade . . . Of course, I had to somehow get that letter into the knothole in the oak tree, but I wasn't going a hundred yards near the swamp until it was full light out. Right after school would be a good time.

I spent the day in near silence, and Robyn and Tully thought I was still moping after Clay. Good. It meant they would leave me alone. Not that I didn't want the company of my friends. More like I might burst into tears or snap at them because of all the stress I was under. I didn't need to ostracize myself even more.

Tully drove me home that afternoon, and I was glad that she took me all the way to the end of the road.

"Thanks Tully," I mumbled as I climbed out of her dad's car.

"Hey Meg,"

I paused. There was real concern in her voice. She never let her concern show. I turned, trying to put on a nonchalant face. I think I might have failed a little.

"You know you can talk to me, about Clay, about anything."

Tully was reaching out, and as much as I wanted to just fling myself against her shoulder and cry, I couldn't. I couldn't confide in her. It was too dangerous. I had no idea, really, what was out to get me but there was no way in hell I was going to let it get Tully.

Taking a deep mental breath, I shrugged and said, "No, I'm okay Tully, really I am. There are some things going on right now that are just stressing me out. I'll be fine. I promise."

Tully grinned, her pale green eyes looking a bit sad. "Okay, but you know where to come if you need a shoulder."

I smiled, despite my sudden melancholy. I knew I could always count on Tully.

I watched her car disappear down the street before I dug my hand into my backpack and pulled out the note to Cade. I shaded my eyes and looked up into the canopy of the eucalyptus trees. The sun was far from setting and it wasn't going to get any brighter. Leaving my backpack on our front porch, I ran to the end of our street, slipped past the fence marking the dead end, and sprinted to the oak tree several yards away.

Stepping up onto the roots and reaching around the back, I located the knothole and quickly shoved the note in. I didn't even check to make sure the end wasn't sticking out. I raced back up the equestrian path and out onto the road, turning left up our driveway. Breathing heavily from my frantic run, I scooped up my backpack, fished out my house key, and let myself in.

I waved to my mom, who was sitting on the living room floor with Aiden, Joey and Jack, helping them put together a giant jigsaw puzzle.

"Hi hon," was all she said. "Frantic day at school?"

Betrayed

Oh. She must have been referring to my disheveled look.

I shrugged and grinned. It was hard keeping all my secrets from my family, but luckily I was in high school and they expected some level of aloofness.

"Yeah, had a pretty strenuous P.E. class today."

Mom waved me on, knowing I would have homework to do. I headed downstairs and once there I pulled out my books. But once again, homework was the furthest thing from my mind. I wondered when Cade would get my message, *if* Cade would get my message. I sighed and got back to geography. Best not to think about Cade or the Otherworld right now.

Three days later I got home from school to find Fergus sitting at my door, panting and grinning like always.

I cried in surprise and delight. The note! Cade must have left me another message. For a minute, I was giddy. Then my spirits dropped. What if he didn't want to meet with me? What if he had received my note, but was only writing back to tell me to leave off?

I bit my lip. I dreaded going down to the oak tree now, but not because I feared the faelah that could be waiting for me. I was afraid Cade might have rejected me.

Stop it Meghan. Rejected or not, you need to know.

Steeling myself, I grabbed my shoes and shoved them onto my feet. I threw open my door and jogged after Fergus as he loped down the horse path towards the oak tree. I nearly tripped on a tree root in my haste to get to the note. Must have been my nerves.

I slipped the note from its hiding place and with trembling fingers I unrolled it, scanning my eyes across the sparse words.

Meghan,
I will meet you tomorrow afternoon in the clearing.
C.M.

Faelorehn

I slumped my shoulders in disappointment. Okay, well at least it wasn't a rejection. But I had hoped there would be more to it than that.

The note's brevity had my mind occupied all the way to my room, so I didn't notice the looming raven until I was just outside my door. It startled me at first, like it always did, but this time it seemed only to be watching me. I wanted dearly to throw a rock at it, but I had no idea what powers this particular faelah might possess and the last thing I wanted to do was anger it. Quickly, I stepped inside my room and locked my door behind me, closing the blinds as an extra measure.

The next day, I got a ride home with Thomas right after school. I had tried to present a more cheerful face during the day and Tully seemed to be a little more relaxed. That was a good sign, I thought. I had contemplated just walking home that afternoon, taking the back way and waiting for Cade, but as silly as it was, I wanted to go home and make myself more presentable first.

I stepped into my bathroom and pulled out the makeup I kept stowed in the top drawer. The last time I'd used any serious amount of it had been for the dance on Halloween. I carefully applied some mascara, lip gloss and eyeliner. I tried to ignore the changeability of my eyes, if only for the simple reason that their inability to make up their mind on a single color was dizzying. It was a good thing that on a normal day they didn't change this frequently. People were more comfortable accepting that it was the lighting that made them seem to switch from hazel, to grey, to blue.

Once satisfied with my makeup, I fiddled with my hair a little. It had a bit of curl to it today, and I opted to keep it down. I didn't leave my hair down that often because it got in the way. This afternoon I thought it might make me look more fetching. Ha. *Me,* fetching . . .

Betrayed

Finally, I changed into my good jeans and a nice blouse, not my usual t-shirt. Perhaps if Cade were thinking of disappearing for good I might be able to change his mind. I glanced at the mirror hanging on the back of my door. *Well Meghan, it is an improvement, but I don't think you're going to impress Cade.* I heaved a sigh. It was worth a try at least.

Fergus was sitting outside my door when I stepped out of the bathroom, patient as a marble statue. I smiled, despite myself. The dog, um, *spirit guide*, had grown on me, even if he never really showed any emotion.

Our trek into the swamp was a slow one, what with me trying to smooth my nerves and Fergus retreating into his silence. About halfway down, he pulled ahead and started sniffing around in the bushes. To flush out faelah waiting to ambush us? I didn't let it worry me too much. After witnessing his attack on the goat-man, I felt quite safe when Fergus was around, even when he was out of eyesight.

Eventually, the path curved and the small land bridge crossing the swamp came into view. Just a hundred yards or so more. My heart started to flutter and my legs suddenly felt weak. How could Cade have such an influence over me? The willows acted like a screen as I moved closer to the clearing, but just before I stepped out into view I spotted something that made me stop dead in my tracks.

Cade was already there, standing with his back to me and facing a woman. An incredibly beautiful woman. I felt my mouth go dry. She wasn't as tall as me, but her presence oozed extreme confidence. Her hair was jet black and fell in perfect ringlets halfway down her back, and her skin was an almost unearthly pale. On most people it would be considered a flaw, but on her it only seemed to enhance her beauty. Her figure, well, I wasn't exactly flat-chested, but she had the clear advantage over me. She had on a pair of designer jeans that clung to her figure and a shimmery top that accentuated all of her assets without being too revealing.

In a nutshell, she looked like she had just stepped off of the pages of a fashion magazine.

I told myself not to overreact. Clearly she was Faelorehn, for she had that irresistible aura about her that also hung around Cade. I just hoped she was a cousin or a friend. At some point in time the roaring in my ears faded and I got over my numb shock. Breathing slowly through my nose, I inched forward, being careful to stay hidden behind the trees, and strained to hear what they were talking about. It was Cade's voice I picked up first.

"You're leaving. Right now."

Cade grabbed the woman's arm roughly and tried to move her towards the path leading to the dolmarehn. Anger, and maybe even a bit of fear, seemed to roll off of him in waves.

"I will not have you here when Meghan arrives."

The beautiful woman only laughed; a cruel, confident laugh that made the hair on my arms rise.

"Oh? And why's that Cade? Don't want your little *Faelorah* to know about the most important woman in your life?"

Cade froze, pausing in his attempt to get the woman to leave. I tensed. *Oh Meghan, you have been so utterly stupid!* I gritted my teeth and willed the tears forming in my eyes to evaporate. But it was no use. I just hoped Cade and his, *girlfriend* (for who else could she be after a statement like that?), couldn't hear my heart breaking.

It felt as if the earth were opening up beneath me, to swallow me and put an end to my misery. Of course, Cade and his companion didn't notice. The woman sneered and yanked her arm free. Cade did nothing to stop her and through my blurred vision it looked almost as if he had been defeated. Like a dog cowering before its angry master.

"I will remind you, Cade dearest, that I am the one who gives orders and when they are not followed . . ."

I didn't stay to hear the rest; I was too distraught. I had to get out of there before I started sobbing and drew attention to myself. I knew this had been a possibility from the get-go. I knew

Cade might already be spoken for. But it still hurt; it still dug at my heart.

I practically ran all the way back to my room, sobbing the entire way, my carefully applied makeup now streaming down my face. I threw open my sliding glass door, slammed it shut behind me and locked it. I didn't even bother changing or washing my face before I fell onto the top of my bed to cry into one of my pillows.

Logan called down the stairs to say that dinner was ready, and fortunately I had enough energy to call back up that I wasn't feeling very well and that I was going to bed early. No one came to investigate. Thank goodness. Rolling over on my back, I stared at the ceiling and let my misery flood over me. Eventually I fell asleep, but only because I was so exhausted. I didn't even notice when Fergus returned to my back door to lie down and fall asleep.

Eighteen
Heart-broken

I was sick over what I had discovered, so sick that I stayed home the next day. I had acted like one of those stupid jealous girls you see on TV or in a movie, the ones who allow their lives to revolve around their perfect guy. I winced. At least I had left before I made a scene. What had happened to me? I had always been the sensible one. Why had I fallen so hard for Cade? The realization of that fact, and the fact that I had finally admitted that what I suffered from was far worse than some crush, rocked me and turned me over like that time I tried kayaking at the beach. I sat up in bed, my mind nearly blank with shock, as one resounding thought reverberated around in my skull. I was in love with Cade MacRoich.

I grabbed a pillow and shoved my face into it, groaning. Oh, this was not good. He had a girlfriend, one who was way prettier than I was. Worse, a girlfriend he never mentioned to me. *Because you are so far from being a possible match for him, Meghan, that he didn't even bother dishing out that information.* It didn't matter that I was Faelorehn like him; that I had finally found someone who didn't think I was some freak of nature. Hot tears burned my eyes and spilled out to stain my pillowcase.

Oh Meghan, don't you see now? All that stuff he told you about being half Fomorian and half Tuatha De? Either he had been lying about all that and had only been trying to get rid of me, or it was still true and he no longer wanted to have anything to do with me because of it. I had always wondered if my body could produce only a limited amount of tears. I was starting to fear I might be putting that theory to the test.

When my depression passed and my mind cleared, I took a deep breath and tried to shove the image of Cade from my thoughts. It was too early to contemplate all the possible meanings of what I'd witnessed yesterday. Best to distract myself with sleep.

The next morning I got up and got ready for school. I still felt terrible, but I needed to start functioning again. Tully noticed something was wrong right away but luckily I had the excuse of getting over my illness to explain away my groggy, gloomy mood. Sometimes she was too perceptive.

The day passed slowly and I hardly took note of my classes. Coach Tillmann even let me sit out during P.E., claiming I still looked rather sickly. His idea of curing the flu was to go into the weight room and do as many bench presses as humanly possible. The fact that he was extending his sympathy my way wasn't a good sign. Time to ditch my drama queen act and get over it pronto. Only problem was, that was easier said than done.

I accepted a ride home from Robyn that afternoon and thanked my lucky stars she was in one of her self-centered moods. She spent the entire three minutes it took her to get to my driveway complaining about the streak of green in her hair.

"It's teal, not lime. Honestly, how can the color description be that far off?"

I merely shrugged as I yanked my backpack from the backseat. I shut the passenger side door, more forcefully than I had meant, and the partially rolled-down window rattled in its frame.

"Uh," Robyn said, eyeing me for what seemed like the first time that day. "You okay? You seem more depressed than sick."

I gritted my teeth. "I'm fine. Just had a headache all day and my stomach hasn't quite settled yet."

Not exactly a lie.

"Well, you'd better get inside and within puking range of a toilet then, just in case. Hope you feel better tomorrow!"

Robyn threw her car into drive and practically peeled out down our quiet road. I sighed and glanced around our driveway. It was empty. If I was lucky, no one would be home yet.

I bypassed our front door and went straight to the backyard, unlocking my sliding glass door with the proper key and slipping inside, closing and locking it behind me. I dropped my backpack in a corner and belly flopped onto my bed. I wanted at least an hour of peace before my brothers and my parents got the chance to bother me.

I must have dozed off, because all of a sudden I was staring at my alarm clock and it was two hours later than it had been a few minutes ago. I dragged myself off of my bed, feeling grumpy and rumpled and wondering why I felt so forlorn. Then it came back to me: staying home the day before, walking around in a daze all day long at school, realizing I had fallen for the strange guy who claimed to be from the Otherworld . . . I groaned and scrubbed my face with my hands.

"Meg! Mom says dinner's ready!" one of my brothers called from upstairs.

I sighed, did a quick check in my bathroom mirror, and plastered a smile on my face. The last thing I wanted was for my family to know I was pining after some guy. Giving myself one more power talk, I climbed the stairs to join them for dinner.

That entire week consisted of me gradually convincing myself that learning about Cade's girlfriend was a good thing and that my broken heart would mend within the month. But as each day passed, I yearned to see him, or simply get a note from him. I wanted an explanation of who the woman was, even though I already knew. I wanted to hear it from Cade. And besides, I had taken off that day without ever letting him know I had been there in the clearing. Surely he was just as curious as I. Didn't he want to know why I never showed up? I squashed that thought right away. *He doesn't feel the same way about you Meghan. After that fight with his girlfriend, he probably forgot all about you.*

"What's been up with you lately? You're not sick again, are you?" Tully asked around a mouthful of tuna salad sandwich.

"Huh?" I blurted, snapping out of my daze. I sighed, twirling my cold spaghetti salad with my fork. "Oh. Nothing. I'm fine." I tried a smile, but it felt very foreign to me.

Robyn stared at me. "Nothing? Are you serious? You've been walking around as if you are living in a different dimension all week!"

I cringed. If she only knew how accurate she was . . .

"Just ready for summer, that's all."

"Most people who are ready for summer are antsy. Hyped up and talking about the beach and the lake," Will commented as he polished off a soda.

"You're acting as if . . ." Robyn trailed off and her eyes grew wide. "Meghan, you're acting as if you've got it bad for some guy! Is it Clay again?"

The blush that flooded my face responded automatically and completely without my permission.

"Who's Clay?" Thomas asked.

"Meghan? Is this why you've been acting so distant for the past month?" Tully asked gently.

I had totally forgotten about the fabricated Clay, but I wasn't in the mood to talk about any guy, invented or real.

"No!" I said in response to my friends' questions. I scooped up the remains of my lunch and headed towards the closest trash can. "There's no one!"

After getting rid of my lunch, I merely walked away, leaving my four friends to gawk after me in shock. I didn't want to talk to them about Cade. How would I explain everything to them without sounding like I'd finally gone off the deep end? I was so glad that I wouldn't be seeing them for the rest of the day and that it was a Friday. I could use the weekend to recover my bearings and maybe come up with some excuse or story to tell them.

I had been avoiding the swamp all week, but today I decided it was best if I take the back way home and take my chances. If Tully and Robyn couldn't find me in the parking lot after school, then they couldn't force me to talk about Cade.

Walking through the swamp and the surrounding woods had been a bad idea. Hadn't I been trying to forget about Cade? So why did I decide to take a nice little stroll through the place that reminded me of him the most? A wave of emotion swept over me: anger, mostly at myself for falling for someone so utterly unattainable, regret and fear that I might not ever see him again, and a bone-deep sorrow for the whole entire, stupid, messy situation.

As I plodded down the road, slipping a little on the gravel as the steep asphalt became a wide dirt path, my roiling emotions came to a breaking point and a sudden anger surfaced above them all. How dare Cade lead me on like that, treating me with more kindness and caring than any guy had ever done before him? Even Thomas and Will considered me to be just one of the guys, not that I'd ever consider dating either of them. Thomas for obvious reasons and Will just wasn't my type. But Cade?

I wrapped my arms tightly around myself as the dirt path brought me to the outskirts of the swamp. I could see the small bridge of land that crossed its shallowest point just a few yards ahead. Cade *had* been interested in me, hadn't he? My anger at him soon turned into anger at myself. Perhaps I had read too much into his actions and words. Perhaps things were done differently in the Otherworld.

"Hello Meghan."

Heart-broken

I screamed at the sound of the unfamiliar voice and only because my thoughts were so lost elsewhere. Turning with wide eyes, I found someone standing in the clearing that had become such a familiar meeting ground for me. As soon as I saw who it was, I gaped in shock. It was the beautiful Faelorehn woman, this time wearing a summer dress and heels. Really? Heels? In the swamp? I snorted. Why was that the thought that came to my mind? This was Cade's girlfriend; shouldn't I be more concerned with why she was here, talking to me?

The woman crossed her arms and smiled, her crimson lips and violet eyes making her white skin seem even paler. I shivered, despite the warm spring air. She simply gave me the heebie-jeebies.

After some time, she released a sigh and started examining the fingernails on her right hand.

"So . . ."

She let that word hang in the air for a while. "Cade has told me all about you."

My stomach dropped. Oh no, was I to be one of those girls who gets attacked by a jealous girlfriend? Would I end up on one of those daytime reality talk shows? I fought the urge to run, though I wanted to do nothing other than bolt up the horse trail and head for my room. But I had the uncomfortable feeling that this woman would be able to catch me, heels or not.

"Um, he did?" I finally managed, my voice feeling raspy.

The woman looked at me and although she smiled, that smile didn't reach her unusual eyes. She blinked and they went from violet to a different color; chestnut? It was hard to tell from where I was standing.

"Oh yes. He informed me that he had found a lost Faelorehn, and that he was determined to teach you all about the Otherworld so that you could be returned home someday."

I felt myself relax, but only a tiny bit. What did she want?

"You're his girlfriend, right?" I blurted. Then I bit my lip. *Stupid.*

The woman threw her head back and laughed, a genuine laugh this time, and her black, curly hair bounced with the movement. When she recovered and looked back at me, her eyes seemed to sparkle.

"Oh yes, we do have quite an *intimate* relationship."

I blushed and tried not to think about just how intimate. Ugh, could my situation get any worse? As if on cue, my eyes started to prick. No! I would not cry in front of her! I managed to resist breaking down, but just barely.

"Well, it was nice meeting you, but I really should get home. My family will be wondering where I am."

I turned to walk away, clutching the straps of my backpack to keep a hold of my emotions.

"Wouldn't you like to come see the Otherworld, though? I can take you now if you'd like. Would only take a few minutes."

I froze. Why did she want to take me to the Otherworld? I turned and arched a brow.

She shrugged sheepishly. "Cade asked me to do him a favor. Said he couldn't cross over for a while and asked me to bring you to him on the other side. He spoke so fondly of you, like you were a sister to him."

I winced and felt terrible all over again. He thought of me like a sister? That was worse than him having a girlfriend. But . . . it was tempting. To see Cade again, even if just for a few minutes, and even if he already had a girlfriend. Maybe I could bring closure to my pointless feelings. Maybe if I saw them together as a couple, I could finally move on. It still hurt worse than anything in the world, but at least I would never be left to remain wondering . . .

"Okay," I sighed.

I began to step towards the woman, but at that second Fergus came trotting out of the willows. I expected him to come stand by me or maybe run up to the woman with his tail wagging. Surely the hound would be familiar with her. Instead, he did something that surprised me, and frightened me a little. He came to stop just in front of me and took on a defensive stance. With hackles raised, he released a low warning growl and locked eyes with the Faelorehn fashion model standing only fifteen feet in front of me.

Blinking in surprise, I took my eyes off of Fergus and looked up at the woman. She looked . . . nervous? Annoyed? Both maybe? I couldn't tell, but it was obvious she wasn't going to get anywhere near Fergus. That was odd.

"It's okay Fergus," I said, "she's going to take me to Cade."

Had Cade somehow asked his spirit guide not to let me go to the Otherworld? So he wouldn't have to deal with me anymore? No, that didn't seem right. He may have broken my heart, but Cade had always been a gentleman. Then what was wrong?

"Oh, silly Fergus. He does that sometimes," the woman trilled. "I think he's jealous of me."

Giving that cool smile, she strode forward, her gate as smooth as a swan's. Fergus lunged and snapped, barking and snarling.

I stepped back in shock. The only time I had ever seen him act out in aggression was when those Cúmorrig attacked, and when the goat-man came after me.

I looked up at Cade's girlfriend. Yep. She was definitely irritated. Her eyes flashed dangerously and her beautiful mouth curved down in a frown. But she didn't try to move any closer.

I placed my hand on Fergus's neck, shushing him and speaking quietly. "Calm down Fergus, don't you recognize her?"

The hound glanced back at me and something crossed over his eyes. A memory came to mind, a memory of a conversation with Cade. And then I could have sworn I heard his voice in my head.

"Don't trust anyone who claims to be Faelorehn."

I glanced back up at the woman standing before me. Sure, she hadn't claimed to be Faelorehn, but it was pretty obvious. And if she was Cade's girlfriend, shouldn't she be trustworthy?

Fergus's sudden growl told me no. But could I just walk away nonchalantly after agreeing to go to the Otherworld with her? *Time to think fast Meghan.*

"You know what, maybe I should wait on going to the Otherworld. Fergus seems a bit upset and I don't want him to attack either of us. Besides, my parents expect me to check in after school before I go out. Can I take a rain check?"

I put on my best smile, all the while clinging to Fergus's rough fur. It made me think of the little girl I'd been on the streets of L.A., using the white hound as my anchor.

At first, the woman looked as if she was seconds away from throwing a major tantrum, but then she closed her eyes slowly and took a few deep breaths. When she opened them, they were once again a cool violet color. She put on a smile, this one looking genuine, and shrugged her shoulders.

"Very well. I wouldn't want to get you in trouble. However," she paused. Suddenly the light in her eyes faded and she choked back a sob.

I blinked in surprise.

"I didn't want to say anything," she whispered, tears streaming down her face. She looked up at me with imploring eyes. "But, I'm afraid Cade's in a lot of trouble. The last job he took on, well, I think it was too much for him. You have no idea what power the faelah wield in our world."

Oh, I had an idea, if I was judging by Cade's haggard appearance the last few times I had seen him. But her obvious fear and the information she had just given me sent a pang to my heart. Cade was in trouble.

"And he's certain that you have some hidden power that will awaken in the Otherworld and help him defeat these monsters. But, oh, he told me not to say anything to you." She choked back another sob. "He thought it was possible you could help him, but he doesn't want to risk you getting hurt. Oh Meghan," she looked up at me with wide, frightened eyes, "I promised I wouldn't tell you any of this, but I'm so worried that he won't survive the fight this time unless someone can help him. If it is true, what he told me about you, that you are descended from a Fomorian and a Tuatha De, then you could be the only one who can save him."

I felt my fingers tighten even more in Fergus's fur. Had Cade been trying to protect me all along? Was he now on the verge of death, simply to keep me safe? All of a sudden, all of my anger, all of my sorrow fled with the wind. A warm contentment filled me, but soon it was replaced by fear. Cade needed my help.

Fergus growled again, but I ignored him.

"I'll come," I said, my voice harsh with determination, "but I have to go home first and tell my parents I'm going out for the night."

Cade's girlfriend heaved a great sigh of relief. "Thank you," she breathed, looking slightly haggard herself. "I must go now, to see if I can aid him until you get there. Do you know where the dolmarehn is, to get to the Otherworld?"

I nodded.

"Good. Just pass through the cave and I will meet you on the other side. From there, we can find Cade and hopefully, if it's not too late, save his life."

I turned to go. I had to get back to the house as quickly as possible and let my parents know I'd be out for a while. I could have gone with her right then and there, but Mom and Dad would worry and I didn't want to put them through that.

"Meghan?"

I turned to see the beautiful woman gazing at me, her face a mask of worry.

"Thank you."

Faelorehn

I nodded at her, then turned and sprinted up the horse trail that would bring me home. I didn't know how much time Cade had, but I was determined to get there before it was too late.

Nineteen

Eilé

C ade had once told me never to go into the cave that led to the Otherworld unless I had no other choice. Well, at the moment I really didn't have any other choice. The Faelorehn woman (ugh, why hadn't I asked her name?) had told me Cade was in trouble. In my book a friend in trouble required me to call upon desperate measures, especially since I couldn't do anything as simple as call the police. Of course, I could be walking straight into a hostile environment, but I was beyond caring for the time being.

A fog had blown in towards the end of the day, as if it knew what I was up to and was only helping to set the mood. Mom and Dad hadn't been home yet when I made it back to the house, so I left them a note about going out with friends and that I would be back very late. I hoped whatever it was I was supposed to do to help Cade didn't take all night. I made sure to have my cell phone on me, but I had a feeling that I wouldn't get service in the Otherworld.

I shook my head and took a deep breath, puffing a little as I walked up the trail that would eventually plunge back down into the culvert where the dolmarehn was located. I was so fixated on going through with this; of walking into that cave and crossing over into the Otherworld, that I hadn't noticed the sudden silence of the woods or the eyes that watched me from the overgrowth. I was so busy trying to ignore the warning voice in my head that told me I was acting too rashly, that I hadn't thought this through, that I didn't see the great black raven watching me with fire in its eyes.

Taking one more deep breath and pulling my thin jacket over my shoulders, I stepped over the broken branches and pushed aside the tree roots hanging in front of the cave like a screen. Shutting my wayward thoughts out of my mind, I stepped out of the white fog and into the blackness of nothingness.

My first impression of the cave to the Otherworld was total darkness. I blinked a few times, stretching my arms out tentatively in front of me. I nearly screamed when my trembling fingers brushed against something soft and stringy. After a few seconds of consideration, I realized it was only more roots hanging from the cave ceiling. It was a small space, after all, only just big enough for a normal sized adult to pass through without much trouble. Cade must have had to duck and make himself as small as he could whenever he passed this way.

The sudden thought of Cade rubbed painfully against my raw emotions. Some of my anger towards him started to fade away and my more compassionate side kicked in. Maybe he hadn't wondered about my missed meeting because he had been in trouble. I hadn't thought of that before. My stupid, selfish teenage heart was only concerned about its own welfare. Now I was beginning to worry. I picked up my pace, keeping my fingers crossed there weren't any really big spiders in here or sudden drops that might result in a sprained ankle.

As I felt my way through the cave, using the wall to my right as a guide, I breathed deeply to keep my heartbeat at a normal pace. The air smelled and tasted like dust, mildew and eucalyptus oil at first, but after several minutes the temperature dropped dramatically and a cool, moist breath of air slithered past my face and caused the hairs on the back of my neck to stand on end. The scent of rain and wet stone and something that just felt ancient flooded my nose, and the darkness around me seemed to grow blacker. I started to shiver and I wanted to wrap my arms tightly around myself, but I was afraid to take my fingers from the earthen wall. I imagined that just a few small steps ahead of me there lay a great abyss, deeper than the earth itself, ready to swallow me whole.

I should have turned around then and there and gone straight home to think this whole hare-brained idea over again. After all, the only information I had to go on had been delivered by a Faelorehn woman I'd never met before. How did I know she wasn't trying to make a fool out of me? *Go home Meg,* I told myself, *go home and think about this. Cade may need your help, but at least go back home and get your bow and arrows.*

Cursing silently to myself for being so scatter-brained that I'd forgotten the very weapon I could use to fight the faelah, I started to turn and head back out the way I had come. I didn't even get the chance to see the light pouring from the mouth of the cave several feet away. Something caught me and refused to let go. It wasn't anything physical; it was as if some sixth sense inside of me had magnetic qualities and that another magnet, located in that great void I was sure stood gaping in front of me, had sensed its presence and was pulling it forward.

The sensation grew stronger and soon I felt myself being dragged forward. I grasped at the wall with my hands but it was no use. With a great cry and a rush of fear, the cold air intensified and swallowed me whole. To my great relief, I blacked out before I could experience anything else.

I can't say how long I was out, nor can I describe the strange and terrifying dreams that haunted me while I lay unconscious. All I can say is that some undeterminable amount of time after being sucked into that black, cold void inside the cave, I woke up gasping for air as if I had stopped breathing altogether.

Faeborehn

My head was killing me, I felt like I was going to throw up, and if I hadn't known any better, I would have sworn I'd been in a horrible car accident. Every bone in my body hurt. I had no idea human beings had so many bones. Oh wait, scratch that, I wasn't a human being.

Groaning, I tried to sit up. I still hadn't opened my eyes. My eyelids were too tired to lift. Thick, damp, soft moss or grass gave under the pressure of my hand and a cool mist caressed my skin like a chilly blanket. I managed to push myself back a little, my shoulders coming into contact with what felt like a great granite gravestone. My stomach lurched again and fear shivered down my spine. If I was in a graveyard, I think I might just faint.

Finally, I managed to crack my eyes open, then blinked in surprise at what I saw. The sky was thick with heavy mist, but all around me, in a large circle, were tall, natural pillars of granite.

At first I had the ridiculous notion that the dolmarehn I had entered had thrown me onto the Salisbury Plain and smack center within Stonehenge, but as my senses returned I realized that that couldn't be right and for a few reasons. First, I could almost see the tops of these stones and the monoliths at Stonehenge were much taller. Second, the circle couldn't be more than fifteen feet in diameter. Third, and this was when that fear started clenching my stomach again, there was a gateway directly across the circle from me.

I knew it was a gateway because it had to be where I'd come from. It looked like those stone dolmens you see on the covers of photography books featuring Ireland; two large slabs of rock topped with a third, creating a doorway. This doorway was pressed into the side of a small hill and yawned black and menacing, as if the stones were merely outlining some deep cave. Above it, on the hilltop, stood an old gnarled oak tree.

Glancing around, I noticed more oak trees. I came to the conclusion that this gateway to the Otherworld sat on the highest point in the middle of a small oak grove, for the quiet trees stood all around, their eerie silhouettes scattered about in the fog.

I took a deep breath and scooted myself further up into a sitting position, using the closest stone as a backrest. It dawned upon me then that maybe I had been launched out of the dolmarehn and slammed up against this rock. That would explain the full-body ache. But why was I here . . . ? Oh right, *Cade*.

A quiet rustling soon drew my attention away from everything else. I squinted into the fog, my heart pounding as I wondered what might have caused the sound. Out of the mist, a black shape swooped down from the oak tree above the Otherworldly gate and came to rest atop one of the stone monoliths. It bent its neck and let out a long, mournful caw, sending goose bumps up my arms. It was the raven that had been stalking me for the past several months, I was certain.

In the next breath, the bird swooped down to join me and as it descended the strangest thing happened. Its feathers melted away and its legs grew longer. It was morphing into a figure before my very eyes, and by the time it landed on the ground it had become a woman dressed all in black. Her transformation from bird to woman had been so smooth and flawless that all I could do was gape. Yet, that wasn't the only reason I was gaping. As she approached I got a good look at her face. Pale white, flawless skin, obsidian black hair, blood-red lips and violet eyes. It was the Faelorehn woman who had begged for my help: Cade's girlfriend.

"Hello Meghan," she said in a frighteningly calm voice. "I am so glad you could finally make it. Welcome to Eilé."

I can't say how I did it, but somehow I managed to speak, asking the question I should have asked to begin with, "Who are you?"

She crossed her arms and arched one of those perfect eyebrows. If anything, her unearthly beauty and overwhelming presence was magnified here, on this foggy, wooded hillside full of stone columns.

"Oh, I have a few names," she said nonchalantly. "Some call me Neaim, others Macha. I've also gone by Badb on occasion."

I was confused. There was something familiar about those names, but I just couldn't put my finger on it. I think it had mostly to do with my aching head, but I must admit a good deal of it was because of the fear I felt brewing in my heart. This woman was dangerous. I could feel that more than ever now, as if she had a hurricane brewing within her and she was just waiting to unleash it at the right time.

"But," she continued, "you might know me best as the Morrigan."

And at that moment it dawned upon me just how stupid and suicidal crossing into the Otherworld had really been.

"Where is Cade?" I whispered, my head lowered so she wouldn't see my fear. *The Morrigan was Cade's girlfriend!?* Just how much had he been keeping from me? And who must he be to be dating one of the most powerful of the Celtic deities?

"I have sent him off on a tedious mission so that we might have a little one on one time together," the woman, no, the *goddess*, answered. "You see, I've been looking for you for a long time Meghan, and he was supposed to bring you directly to me if he ever found you. But he was becoming distracted, so naturally I reassigned him. Sorry about that little fib earlier, but you really were being very difficult. I had to get you to cross over somehow."

Wait, *what?* What was she talking about? She had been looking for me? Oh wait, she was the raven . . . But *why* had she been looking for me? And what did she mean Cade was getting distracted? By what? And how had she reassigned him? I braved a glance at her, but her eyes were unreadable. Terrifying, sadistic and now those very eyes were phasing from violet to crimson.

Éilé

"What sort of mission did you send him on?" I braved, my voice quavering a little. "And what do you want with me?"

The last conversation I'd had with Cade came screaming back into my mind. *Some people would rather see you dead than risk learning whether or not you are a threat.*

Oh Meghan, what have you done . . . ?

"This conversation grows tiresome," the Morrigan said rather boorishly, "time to finish the job Cade failed to do. Silly, sentimental little boy," she continued as if I wasn't there anymore. "I really must have a word with him about that."

She started to wander off, the skirts of her black dress taking on a life of their own, stirring and mixing with the mist around her feet. I realized they were made of shadow and smoke and something else . . . death.

"Wait!" I croaked, reaching out with a trembling hand. What did she mean finish the job Cade had failed to do? And how could he be with someone like her? True, she was a beautiful goddess, but from what I'd learned from my research, she loved nothing more than to reign down war and strife upon those she ruled over. How could the Cade I know, the thoughtful, caring Cade, care about someone so twisted and cruel? *Because you don't really know him at all, do you Meghan?* a little voice inside me said. *Perhaps he's been playing you all along . . .*

Despite my wretched state, my stomach had the nerve to give off a twinge of pain and regret when I conjured Cade to my thoughts. I knew my conscience was right, that Cade had probably used me, but it still hurt nonetheless.

The Morrigan turned her head and peered back at me from over her shoulder, her perfectly plucked, black eyebrow arched in annoyance once again.

"No, you miserable *fae strayling*, you do not address me," she all but hissed. "I am the Queen of Darkness and I have decided you may no longer exist."

Faeborehn

Real fear gripped me then, not just at this terrifying being's words, but at the fact that she seemed to grow larger in size, the darkness she so claimed as her own spreading out from her like a black mist to dance and mingle and curl along the ground and in the trees surrounding us.

I could have sworn I heard voices whispering then.

Beware Meghan! Beware! they seemed to say.

It took me a whole five seconds to realize it was the oak trees.

Beware Meghan! they warned. But I was afraid it was too late.

The Morrigan closed her eyes and let her shoulders relax; her arms to drift away from her body. She lifted her face to the grey sky and began chanting, a deep, resonant melody that made my blood freeze and my breath catch. The words she spoke were ancient, archaic, and although I couldn't understand them, I knew their meaning.

The earth beneath me trembled slightly and the oaks, once so still and solemn in the mist, began quaking as if in fear. The sound of splitting rocks filled the air and the clouds above began to swirl. I decided right then and there that this whole strange scene had to be just another nightmare. Only, this one felt real.

A strange crackling began to blend with the cacophony of chanting, rumbling and rustling, and when I dared take a good look at the changing scene around me, I nearly screamed. Dark figures had started crawling from the small middens dotting the hillside, looking like some horrible horde of grotesque cicadas unearthing themselves after their seven years of dormancy.

The creatures that crawled forth out of the earth were something from a horror movie. Some looked like corpses of bony goblins, vaguely resembling human beings. They walked like spiders and insects, ropes of fur and hair hanging from their rotting flesh. Some had violent, red eyes while others seemed to have no eyes at all. Jagged teeth and long snouts, horns and leathery wings adorned the bedraggled gargoyle-like demons. As

Eilé

they drew closer to our stone circle, hissing and spitting and growling in rage, the Morrigan continued her endless chant, her cruel laughter tainting her ancient words as she called upon her minions to do her dirty work. A horrible smell soon followed them and I had to cover my mouth and nose to keep from gagging.

Screaming in terror once again, I tried to scramble to my feet but I think my leg might have been broken. Wincing in pain and fighting back tears, I darted my eyes around to look for something to defend myself with. A chunk of rock, possibly broken during the initial earthquake of the Morrigan's calling, lay within arm's length. I launched myself at it, falling on my stomach. At first I thought to throw it at the closest faelah demon, but then another thought came to mind. If I threw it at the Morrigan, would it distract her?

Without giving it another thought, I drew back and launched the stone with all my might. It flew towards the Celtic goddess but bounced off some invisible force field surrounding her like a bird smacking into a window. She didn't even falter in her chanting. I had wasted a perfectly good projectile and now the creatures were moving closer.

Just then a terrible baying broke through the scratching and hissing of the creatures. My stomach curled up in dread once again. The corpse hounds. The Cúmorrig. I knew that sound well and any shred of hope or bravery I might have had left fled in the next instant.

Swallowing hard and trying to see through the blurry tears pouring from my eyes, I snatched up a fallen oak branch and huddled near the stone slab I had woken up against. I would fend them off as long as I could, but I knew I was a goner. I thought of my family, my mom and my dad and my brothers. They would come home to find me gone without a trace, only a note saying I'd be out late. I would become another one of those lost girls, abducted by aliens or murdered and well disposed of. How long would my family search for me? Would they ever give up, even when they never found me?

Finally, I thought of Cade. Oh how I had trusted him. Why had I trusted him? Why did he have to betray me? I gasped and my sobs grew stronger as the creatures inched closer. The hounds were getting nearer as well and I could hear their yipping as their excitement grew. My impending demise approached, and the Morrigan continued to chant her death song.

The first hound circled and snapped at the closest faelah demon. For a few minutes a fight ensued, but the corpse dog easily won, tearing the wings of the creature to shreds. The sound of its pain made me even more nauseated. The Cúmorrig moved in, panting and growling, squaring its shoulders for attack. I closed my eyes and waited for impact.

A sharp pain in my leg was the first sign my death was occurring. I screamed and beat at the dog with the stick, but it did no good. Like a swarm of sharks waiting for that first drop of blood to hit the water, the other hounds and creatures swarmed in. I felt them tearing at my clothes and hair, the dull sting of their sharp teeth, twisting my arm almost to the breaking point. I screamed and fought back.

Despite the pain, I was able to make contact with the branch and chase off a few, but there were just too many. I felt my strength sapping, but just before I drifted towards unconsciousness, a shout of sheer anger and desperation split the air. The creatures of darkness blanched for a second and the Morrigan's incessant chanting faltered.

I heard a feminine gasp and the rustling of feathers followed by a loud, furious cawing. The dogs began yowling again and I could feel more than see the demons retreating to their holes. They weren't fast enough though, for something terrifying swept into my circle of stones and started to wreak havoc.

I cracked my eyes open as far as they would go and saw the strangest thing in front of me. Of course, it was only my delirium.

Cade was standing there, looking more terrifying than I could ever remember. He seemed to be growing larger, his thick hair forming into spikes, as if some imaginary hand was adding hair gel and forcing it to stand on end. For some reason, the hair stylist decided to add dye to it because I could see beads of dark red gathering at the tips. I chuckled, coughing on blood. Who would want to dye Cade's hair red? It was already that color.

It was when Cade's body started distorting into the most grotesque shapes I had ever seen this side of some zombie apocalypse movie that I decided my brain must be shutting down, and that this was the death throes I had been expecting. It was like watching a car accident in slow motion or witnessing a cartoon character from one of my brother's favorite shows going bonkers. I had no desire to witness it, but like a drug, the macabre scene drew my eye like a moth to the flame.

An unknown amount of time passed and I could no longer see Cade, but I could still hear what was going on. He must have been ripping the Cúmorrig and the demon things apart, because I could hear them wailing and screeching in pain. The racket probably would have hurt my ears, that is, if I could still feel anything. A blur of pale fur swept by, emitting a sharp bark. *Fergus!*

Suddenly, the horrible screeching stopped and all was still. I wondered if Cade and the creatures had killed one another, but a few minutes later I felt the presence of someone or something approach. Someone strong scooped me up and cradled me against their chest. *Cade.* Unfortunately, I was too numb to enjoy the experience, or to remember that he had a girlfriend and that he didn't care about me at all.

"Meghan!" he breathed close to my ear, his voice sounding harsh and broken. "Oh no, stay with me darling girl."

I'll try, I thought, *but I think you're a bit too late.* Why was I being so reasonable? This was the guy who was dating the Morrigan, the same guy who had apparently lied to me. So why didn't I push him aside? Oh yes, that's right; I was in shock and since I probably only had a few minutes left to live, I wasn't about to reject the attentions of the guy I'd been pining after for the last several months. Immortal or not, the faelah had gotten the better of me and I was definitely dying.

Cade gently pushed his hand up against the back of my head, his fingers tangling in my snarled hair. He was saying something against my ear in that archaic language the Morrigan had used and he was planting kisses on my temple. My stomach fluttered. Not with nausea this time, but with a warm joy. Could it really be happening, or was I imaging it?

Oh, please kiss me for real, I thought.

Then I almost felt like laughing out loud, if I were even remotely close to being fully conscious. There I was, dying on the boundaries of some mystical Otherworld, and all I could think about was this dangerous infatuation I had with some Faelorehn hunter who supposedly was in a relationship with a powerful and beautiful Celtic deity. It was official then: my brain must be fading away with the rest of me.

Cade was no longer speaking but his lips were moving from my temple, to my cheek, to the corner of my mouth that wasn't stained with blood, trailing kisses the entire way. I waited for his lips to finally meet mine, but fate was cruel and I died before I could experience that first and last kiss.

Bright lights flashed far above me and it felt like I was floating. I heard urgent voices, shouting and barking out orders. Was I in heaven? Hell? Knowing how my life had been going for the past several months, I wouldn't be surprised if I ended up in either place.

Eventually, the flashing lights stopped and I detected one steady, bright glare. A sting in my arm, the sound of metal clattering on metal, more voices, an incessant beeping sound and then my awareness faded away again.

Eíļé

I woke in a hospital room, completely disoriented and utterly confused. There were hospitals in the afterlife? A nurse came over to check on me, grinning and making some comment about getting my family. I was alive? After all that had happened? Wait, what had happened? I couldn't remember. All I could recall was that I had been so sure I was dying. Guess I'd been wrong.

Mom and Dad looked ragged, as if they had been up a week straight. My brothers came bounding in, all of them either drying their eyes or trying very hard not to burst into tears.

They explained to me that I had been attacked by some stray dogs or coyotes near my high school. A man driving by saw it all and managed to pull the dogs off of me, then drove me to the hospital. My parents were disappointed that he hadn't left his name, but apparently I had been lucid enough to give him my name and address.

I had only been in the hospital for the night, though it felt like a week. I had plenty of bruises, some deep lacerations that needed stitches and my left leg had been fractured. I had also hit my head pretty hard but they patched me up, put a cast on my leg and proclaimed me fit enough to leave the hospital.

Mom set me up in my bed once we got back home and brought me a pitcher of sweetened iced tea with lemons. She positioned the pillows so that I could sit up and read or watch TV or work on the variety of crossword puzzles and word searches she'd gathered for me.

"The doctor said you should take it easy for the next few days to make sure you don't suffer any more after effects of your concussion," Mom said.

I nodded. Just doing that hurt.

She let out a troubled breath and shook her own head. "A pack of dogs, I can't believe it. What is a pack of dogs doing wandering around the neighborhood?"

She sounded so disbelieving, but not in a way that suggested she didn't believe what had happened to me. There were a few junkyards in the industrial neighborhood on the other side of the highway, but they only kept one or two dogs to warn off any miscreants. Most dogs around here were either friendly or fiercely guarded their own yards.

She shook her head again and said, "I just hope Animal Control finds them before they can hurt anyone else."

Her voice was shaky and I knew she was trying hard not to burst into tears. My mom was tough, she had to be with all my brothers, but when something serious happened she let her emotions show.

I sighed and rubbed my arm. It was sore where the IV had been and where the nurses had given me a rabies shot, just to be safe. I grimaced. I couldn't wait until everyone at school heard about that. I predicted a whole new onslaught of nicknames coming my way.

Mom kissed me on the top of my head once more, her eyes shining with the emotion she was trying so hard to keep at bay, and then instructed me to send her a text on her cell phone if I needed anything. I told her I would be fine, but I picked up my phone and held it up to reassure her. Casting me one last smile, she made her way up my spiral staircase and disappeared through the trap door.

Feeling overwhelmingly blessed about my current state of existence, I huffed a great sigh and leaned fully into my pillows. If my parents had any idea what had really happened . . . I screwed up my face. But what exactly *had* happened? It was still all a blur to me, the details at least, but I did recall crossing over into the Otherworld and then being almost immediately attacked by a contingent of monsters. I had done something to defend myself, something pathetic like picking up a rock or a stick. I really needed more practice with the lessons Cade had been giving me.

I cringed at the thought of Cade. Had that really been him when I was certain I was dying? Had he really managed to thwart the Morrigan and chase away her monsters and hounds? Or had

Eilé

that just been another one of my delusions? Had he really held me in his arms and had he truly kissed me before I lost consciousness? And if so, could everything that the Morrigan said to me be a lie? *Duh Meghan, she lured you into the Otherworld to kill you. Time to re-evaluate your opinion about Cade . . . again.*

I sighed and turned my head towards the sliding glass door that looked out into my backyard. It was early evening and the shadows of the trees were painting gray streaks across the lawn. It didn't matter if Cade had come to help me, for I had a terrible feeling I would never see him again.

Tears pricked my eyes and an ache worked its way up into my throat. As I drifted off to sleep, three thoughts surfaced to my mind. First, I prayed to whatever gods existed that the memories of my ordeal wouldn't haunt me during my sleep. Second, I asked those same deities that the Morrigan would think I was dead and therefore wouldn't come back for me. And lastly, I hoped with all my heart that Cade was safe somewhere in the Otherworld. Despite my mixed feelings towards him and regardless of the fact that the Morrigan seemed to have a significant amount of control over him, I only wished him well. Perhaps I really did love him, for why else would I feel this way towards someone who very well may have forsaken me?

Twenty

Explanation

hen I opened my eyes again it was just before dawn. I wasn't sure what had woken me, for the silence in my room and just outside my doors was almost deafening. I had to just lie in bed for a few minutes as my muddled mind resurfaced. The medication they had given me at the hospital must have lingered longer than I thought. Finally, I took a deep breath and glanced towards the glass door. I nearly screamed in surprise.

"Fergus!" I meant to shout, but it only came out as a croak.

The great white wolfhound panted just outside my door, looking like a ghost against the early morning fog. I threw back the covers and made to get out of bed but the cast caught my eye. Ah, yes. Broken leg. Maybe Mom had left me some crutches . . . I looked around then sighed. No luck. I contemplated hop-limping over to the door but as soon as I put pressure on the leg, I cried out in pain.

I sat on the edge of my bed, the sheets thrown back, feeling rather forlorn. I was wearing a pair of boxer shorts bedecked with my favorite cartoon characters from my middle school years and an old, faded t-shirt. I reached up and touched my hair. Yep, it was a mess. I hadn't had a chance to take a good look at the bruises that decorated my face or the stitches in my shoulder and neck, but I'm sure it made me look like some sort of teen version

Explanation

of Frankenstein's monster. *Oh well,* I thought with a grin, *it's only Fergus who's seeing me like this.*

I glanced up, hoping that the hound hadn't left, and then I nearly fell out of bed in shock. Fergus wasn't alone anymore. A tall figure stood at my door, one hand on the hound's head and the hood of his long trench coat pulled up. Of course, the first emotion that rushed through me was relief followed by a tidal wave of mortification. Oh, what a sight I must be! I scrambled to cover myself with my sheets and blanket, well aware of the view Cade surely had been given. *At least the bruises will hide the blush,* I thought in misery.

Cade must have been waiting for something, because he continued to stand at the door, looking straight ahead. I couldn't see his face clearly, but I knew his eyes were trained on me. After a few more seconds I realized he was waiting for me to give him permission to enter my room. My dark, cluttered, too-many-personal-things-left-out-for-him-to-see room. I bit my lip. Should I let him come in? I glanced around in embarrassment. Dirty clothes were scattered everywhere, my desk was untidy and my bathroom could have used a good cleaning. I was dressed in nothing but some unfeminine boxer shorts and a hole-ridden t-shirt, my hair a rat's nest and my face looking like a demented artist's pallet.

I glanced back up again. Cade still stood there but Fergus seemed to have wandered off, perhaps to act as a lookout. I wasn't ready to face Cade yet; at least I didn't think I was. I still wasn't sure what his intentions were. From the beginning he had seemed to be there to help me, but in retrospect, why would he? I was a stranger and his job was to round up wayward Faelorehn and the lost creatures of the Otherworld to bring them back to where they belonged. So why hadn't he done that with me? Why hadn't he returned me to the Otherworld when he had found me to begin with? There had to be a reason and I wasn't sure if I wanted to know that reason yet. The Morrigan could have been lying when she had said something about Cade having a mission, but she also could have been telling the truth.

I sighed. I shouldn't let Cade in but the fact that he was waiting for my permission was a good sign. Besides, deep down, I really wanted to know if that had been him on the other side of the dolmarehn. If he had saved me in the end or if it had just been an illusion on my part. And if he had saved me . . . Well, then perhaps he wasn't as bad as the Morrigan had tried to paint him. And I really wanted to see him again, desperately, if only to hear his voice and simply bask in his presence.

Taking a deep breath, I looked up and nodded once. My door must have been unlocked because he slid it open with a cool swoosh. Funny, I'd been so careful to keep it locked of late . . .

Stepping out of the fog and into my room, Cade delicately pulled back his hood and began to take off his trench coat. He folded it and set it on the small futon against the far wall of my room and padded silently forward. He wore his customary jeans, t-shirt and boots, but there was something about his stance that was off. He was still walking around as if he had been running a marathon every day for the past several weeks.

The lighting was bad in my room, the only brightness coming from the foggy dawn outside and the weak night light in my bathroom. As dark as it was it still couldn't hide the signs of stress on Cade's face. I almost gasped when I finally got a good look at him. He was incredibly pale, much more so than the last time I had seen him. Dark circles shadowed his eyes and his breathing even seemed troubled; shallow and uneven. If I didn't know any better I would have said he'd just been released from a quarantined room after barely surviving a bad case of the Ebola virus.

I cast aside my uncertainty. "Cade," I whispered, reaching out a hand and forgetting about my ridiculous pajamas.

Explanation

He grimaced and avoided my touch. That's right. It wasn't as if he was *my* boyfriend. Who was I to offer comfort?

"I'm so sorry Meghan," he whispered, his voice raspy and full of remorse.

I opened my mouth to argue with him but realized he had said nothing worth arguing with.

He ran his hands over his gaunt face and through his hair. If he had been trying to wipe away his weariness, he had failed.

"This is all my fault." He glanced at my cast-encased leg.

I self-consciously threw my comforter over it and blushed. When had my covers shifted off of me?

"I should have explained more to you, much more, but I didn't think . . ."

He heaved a sigh of frustration and just barely kept himself from punching the wall. He glanced around my room, spotted my desk chair (strewn with all my sweatshirts and jackets) and dragged it over so that he could sit facing me. My wayward clothing fell off in an accusing manner as he pulled the chair in place. He dropped into it, the legs creaking under his weight.

He rested his elbows on his knees and thrust his hands through his hair again, his face bent towards his lap. I got the impression he wanted to pull his hair out.

An eternity seemed to pass and I had no idea what to say, to do, to think. Just a few short hours ago I was sure Cade wanted nothing to do with me, that he had betrayed me and had been using me all along. But his behavior now proved otherwise.

Finally he spoke, though he still sat with his head in his hands.

"You should never have crossed over into the Otherworld."

His statement was so quiet I almost didn't hear him.

"And because I was so arrogant and preoccupied with my own troubles, I never stopped to consider that *she* would figure it out. It's my fault, all my fault."

Faelorehn

I didn't like the way this conversation was going; Cade talking as if I wasn't sitting right in front of him and not explaining anything he was saying. He didn't sound right, as if the weight of the world rested on his shoulders; as if Atlas had given Cade his burden and now he searched me out as someone to confide in. Only, Cade seemed to be confessing, not confiding.

Eventually, he sat up and looked me straight in the eye. His eyes, usually always so dark green, looked impossibly pale now. Pale and empty, just like the rest of him. What had happened to make him look so sickly? A pang of fear shot through me. Yes, I may have been slightly angry with him and terribly confused, but that part of me, the part that created my sentimental emotions, reminded me that no matter what he said or did, I would still love him.

"Meghan, do you know what a geis is?" he finally said.

Uh, *geis?* "No," I answered honestly. To my great relief he elaborated.

"A geis is like a taboo, something that you must never do or else there will be dire consequences. It is prevalent throughout the old Irish folk legends, but it was really a safeguard instituted by the Faelorehn when we first crossed over into this world."

He paused and gave me his characteristic grin. Only, there was too much sadness behind it for me to really enjoy it.

"It kept our kind in check, so that they would not take complete advantage of the human race. It gave us limits, boundaries you could say."

Okay, I think I got all that, but why was he telling me this now?

He gave a huge sigh and when he spoke to me next, he kept his eyes lowered and his voice soft.

"I have a geis, and so do you. Well, I should say we each had a geis."

I felt my mouth go dry. *"Had?"*

Explanation

Cade looked up at me then, his eyes haunted and his mouth grim. He nodded once, and then lowered his eyes again.

"Wait, what do you mean, *had*?"

"You had a geis, and because of me it has been broken."

"What?" I blurted, sitting up straighter. "What do you mean, my geis is broken? How can someone break their geis if they don't even know what it is?"

He grimaced again. "Believe me," he grumbled, "it happens all the time in the Otherworld. Here on earth humanity might call it irony."

My head was spinning again, and not because of the crazy antibiotics and painkillers the doctors had subscribed for my injuries.

"Cade," I licked my lips and swallowed my fear, "please explain. What happens if you break your geis?"

He nodded and took a deep breath. "I never thought you would actually come after me, but I should have seen it coming, especially after I learned who had spoken to you . . ."

I cringed. Oh. So he knew that the Morrigan had paid me a visit? I merely nodded for him to go on, once again hoping my bruises hid my red face.

He sat up fully and drew his shoulders back. He gasped and clutched his arm. Without thinking, I reached out to him again.

"No," he murmured, his eyes drifting shut, "I do not deserve your compassion."

More stung than anything, I let my arm drop, the hurt written all over my battered face.

"When I tell you, you will understand," Cade said as way of an explanation.

"In those first few weeks after I discovered you, I came to suspect there was much more to you than I originally thought, Meghan Elam. When all evidence proved as such, I made it my own personal goal to find out as much about you as I could. I tracked down an acquaintance who was able to help me discover

Faelorehn

who your real parents are. He is the one who suggested you might be Tuatha De and Fomorian. But I have spoken to him since I passed this information on to you, and if he is correct in his most recent discovery, then you are far more than a simple half Tuatha De, half Fomorian castaway stuck in the mortal world."

I felt a strange shock of fear and delight rush through me. Who was I then?

Cade held up a hand. "It's just speculation. We have no real proof yet, but the longer I consider it, the more firmly I believe it."

"Who am I Cade?" I had to know. After learning about the Faelorehn and discovering that I was one of the immortal beings of the Otherworld, I had been dying to know who I was, where I had come from. Who I belonged to.

Cade smiled sadly. "I'm sorry Meghan, but I cannot tell you that. Maybe one day, but not now."

Severe disappointment hit me first, then anger. I crossed my arms and let my chin drop. Tears pricked at my eyes once again.

"I deserve to know," I whispered harshly.

"You do," Cade agreed. "But I cannot tell you. Not now."

He sounded pained, as if he wished to tell me more than anything. Then it dawned upon me.

"Your geis," I said simply. He couldn't tell me because it would break his geis. But hadn't he implied he had already broken it? Yes, when he had been talking about mine.

Cade nodded. "It is more the consequences of my actions. I violated my own geis and now I must pay. One of my punishments includes keeping certain information to myself. I have no control over this."

I looked up at him. "How did you break your geis?" I didn't really expect him to answer, but it didn't hurt to ask.

He took a long, deep breath, as if he were preparing to brace himself against something terribly unpleasant. "I violated my geis the night that you were attacked, but even much longer before that. What the Morrigan said to you that night was true. It was my job to find you and bring you back, though she didn't know it would be you in particular I would find. It was sheer luck that I stumbled upon you. When she found out, she wanted you dead." I gasped and he held up a hand. "Please Meghan, I must tell you this."

I nodded for him to go on, as shocking and frightening as it all was.

"I stalled, tried to change her mind, did everything I could to get her focused on something else. But she wanted you and she wanted you eliminated. It is hard to kill a Faelorehn and only the gods and goddesses themselves cannot die, but I would not kill you Meghan. I *could* not."

He took a deep breath and seemed to become lost for a second. Then he started speaking again. "When she found out I would not follow through with her plans, she distracted me with an assignment in the Otherworld. I *hate* myself for that."

This last part he said so quietly I had to crane my neck to hear it.

"That's when she enticed you into our world, in order to destroy you. For, you see, in doing so your geis was broken."

Ah, so we were back to where we'd started.

Cade glanced up at me, a look of determination on his face. "Meghan, I cannot tell you who you are but I can tell you about the geis that was placed upon you. Your parents knew that someday you would be hunted by the Morrigan, so they did what most of our kind do when their child is in danger because of who they are; they sent you to this world. Now your mother was smart. She not only hid you among the humans of this earth, but she placed a geis upon you. And as you now know, no geis comes without a price."

I nodded, the dread in my stomach starting to coagulate like cottage cheese.

"You would remain safe always from the horrors of the Otherworld, if and only if you never crossed into the borders of

Eilé. So, because of my foolish reluctance to give you certain information, and because of the Morrigan's cruel manipulation, you stepped into the Otherworld and broke your geis."

I didn't know what to say, and if I was being completely honest, I was a bit confused.

"I don't understand," I admitted. "What exactly is, *was*, my geis?"

"Do you remember all the times you were chased or bothered by some Otherworldly creature?" Cade said.

I nodded. How could I forget?

"And did you ever notice how they always stopped short of harming you? As if an invisible shield of protection surrounded you?"

I clenched my hands into fists and thought back. I remembered how the demon goat-man hadn't been able to touch me, how the raven had slammed into not me, but some force field around me. Even the Cúmorrig on that first night I had met Cade . . . Even they hadn't really been able to quite reach me.

Cade nodded solemnly. "You never would have come to harm. Your geis protected you in this world, but since you have crossed over to the Otherworld and stepped foot on Eilé's soil . . ."

"I am no longer protected." I looked up at Cade with wide eyes. "I am now free game." And then something else struck me. "That is why the Morrigan didn't kill me in the clearing. She knew she couldn't hurt me here. She knew she had to get me into the Otherworld, to break my geis, to make me vulnerable. That is why she lured me there, not to help you, but-"

I cut myself short when I noticed Cade start. He was giving me his full attention now, gazing at me with those intense eyes of his. "Help me?"

I blushed. Ugh, why couldn't I stop doing that? I hadn't planned on telling him all that . . . I cleared my throat and sighed. This time I was the one to lower my eyes.

Explanation

"Um, yes. She said you needed my help and that I had some special power or gift that could save you."

Finally I looked up, only to find Cade looking at me in the most bizarre way, as if he were dumbfounded that I would actually enter an unknown world full of monsters in order to help him. Oh yeah, that did sound unbelievable.

He reached out then and took my hand in his own. I was shocked at how cold it was and I almost jerked my own hand away.

"Thank you. I cannot tell you how sorry I am Meghan. You should never have gone with her, but it means a great deal that you would make that sacrifice for me. I don't expect your forgiveness, or your friendship after all this, but I do hope that you know I never meant to harm you."

I nodded, trying to fight the lump in my throat; trying to remember to breathe. Cade had always tried to help me. Despite my current anguish, I was warmed by that thought.

I laughed after a while, though I felt little humor. "I bet your girlfriend is livid with you at the moment. That was you I saw the night she lured me into the Otherworld, right? It was you who fought off the Cúmorrig . . . ?"

But my question trailed off when I felt the bones in my hand begin to constrict.

"Cade, you're hurting me," I said, feeling fear once again. Had I said the wrong thing?

I glanced up at him and the look on his face was something between pure disbelief and . . . disgust?

"Girlfriend?" he said harshly.

"Yes, the Morrigan."

I felt foolish all over again but I managed to get my hand back. Why did I have to go and open my big mouth? Could it be that my brain had stopped working since I found out that I had some semi-important Faelorehn parents who had placed a strong

Faeloreen

geis on me? All after surviving a bizarre, near-death experience? I really needed a vacation away from being me.

Cade was quiet for a long time. "The Morrigan is not my girlfriend. Did she tell you that?"

I bit my cheek. No, she hadn't. But she had implied it.

"I just thought-"

Cade sat up abruptly and looked at me, his gaze hard. I turned away, feeling sheepish. If I blushed any more today my face just might start bleeding. That would be fabulous. Would go well with my stitches and black eye.

Eventually Cade snorted and I was glad to see he had lost that intensity about him. "She *would* want you to think that," he said almost nonchalantly.

"Oh," was all I could say. "But, I saw you in the woods, and I just thought . . ."

"You saw us in the woods?"

Oops times infinity.

While I tried to melt away into oblivion, Cade became still, and then a look of realization spread over his face. "So that is why you never showed up for our meeting," he said quietly. "Meghan," he continued gently, "I can't explain what you saw, like the information about your parents, it's something I must keep to myself. But believe me, the Morrigan is most definitely *not* my girlfriend."

The silence grew between us once again and as I twisted the sheets in my hands, Cade stared down at his interlaced fingers. I could tell he wanted to tell me something more, like lightning charging the air before it struck. I knew it wouldn't be pleasant, but . . . *the Morrigan isn't his girlfriend!* I tried not to let the glee show on my face.

Cade took a breath and released it slowly. "I must go soon Meghan. I violated my geis, and that is no easily forgivable thing."

It had been said so matter-of-factly that I wondered if he had practiced that exact line before he came to see me.

Explanation

I bit my lip to keep it from trembling. "Will I ever see you again?"

"Perhaps. When I've done my penance."

Two days ago I would have bitterly wished him gone from my life for good, but after learning he had made such a sacrifice for me, I didn't want to let him go.

"I brought something for you."

Cade reached around and seemed to pull something out of his back pocket. It looked like a metal cord bent to form a C. The two ends were capped with what appeared to be two hounds' heads in the ancient Celtic style. It looked familiar, like the strange metal choker I'd seen him wear before. I glanced up at him. Yes, almost exactly the same, though the intertwined cord on his was thicker than the one he was holding out to me. For a long time, all I could do was stare at the smaller choker, both transfixed and uncertain. The braided cord was a beautiful silver color and the snarling muzzles of the dogs featured finely etched teeth.

Picking up my hand, Cade drew it towards him and placed the Celtic object in my palm, gently curling my fingers over it. The metal was cold, and so were Cade's hands, but when he let his fingers linger on mine for several seconds, the place where his skin touched mine warmed.

"What is it?" I queried silently.

"It's called a torque." He gestured towards his own. "The ancient Celts wore these into battle. It will protect you while I'm gone."

That's when it hit me. Again. I had broken my own geis, a geis that had acted like some sort of invisible monster repellent. Because of my little side trip into the Otherworld, that repellent was now as useful as hand lotion against the sun's radiation. I didn't even try to stop the tears this time.

"Meghan," Cade breathed quietly, moving his hand to rest against my cheek.

I wanted to move in closer to him, but some deep, primal fear of rejection stopped me. *He's only comforting you Meghan because you are doomed.*

"Meghan, listen to me," Cade continued, wiping my tears away with his thumb. "You are far more powerful than you know and you cannot forget what I have taught you."

I thought back to the archery lessons he had given me down in the swamp. A fresh wave of tears hit when I remembered that that was when I first realized I was falling for him.

"And I'll leave Fergus with you. He'll let me know if you need me."

"Can't I come with you?"

Cade shook his head with a sad smile. "When you crossed over into the Otherworld, the fae power inside of you woke up, like a dormant seed that tastes the first rain of spring and the first warmth of the sun. It shines brightly Meghan, but remember what I told you? Your own power is like a battery run down."

I blinked in surprise. I felt no different than before, but then again I was still pretty sore from the attack.

I furrowed my brow. "But wouldn't it make sense for me to go with you then? So that I can 'recharge'?"

I sounded desperate and I hated that. But to be left here like a sitting duck for the demonic beasts of Eilé to come find me? Surely I was better off with Cade, even if it meant enduring whatever it was he had to do to redeem himself.

"No," he said firmly. "I know it seems like the better option, but even if your fae power were to gain strength, you don't yet know how to use it. I will come back and teach you how to use your gift Meghan, but until then you must stay here. The Cúmorrig and their ilk may seem almost invincible to you here, but they are far more powerful in their natural world. Just remain vigilant and remember what I taught you."

I forced a smile. I was truly touched that he was worried for me, but I still didn't want to think about how long he would be gone and how long I would have to fight off the Morrigan's minions on my own. I took a deep breath and forced my tears to stop. It sucked. This whole situation sucked, but it was high time I stop feeling sorry for myself and take Cade's words to heart. True, I hadn't discovered the depths of my Faelorehn power yet, but if he said it was there then I would believe him.

Smiling, I looked up at Cade. He dropped his hand and smiled back.

"Thank you. For the torque."

I wasn't sure how exactly to wear it, but that was soon resolved when Cade stood and placed it around my neck. The cool metal felt comfortingly familiar, the two hounds' heads growling at each other across my throat.

"It suits you," Cade said with a smirk and a glint in his eyes.

My stomach fluttered again.

He tilted his head and glanced over his shoulder. Fergus stood at my door, panting and wagging his tail slightly.

Cade's shoulders slumped again and he looked back at me. "I must go."

I nodded, dropping my eyes again. *I will not cry . . .*

He turned to leave and I reached out, grabbing his hand. "Cade?"

His eyes were no longer so pale, but they held some emotion I couldn't decipher, yet I knew his attention was fully on me. I should have told him then how I felt about him, that he meant a great deal to me. But I was afraid. Afraid of making myself even more vulnerable.

I cleared my throat. "Be careful, please. And come back soon."

He seemed to pause, as if waiting for me to say more. I'm pretty sure that the slight disappointment I read on his face was just in my mind. Eventually he smiled and nodded ever so slightly.

He took back his hand, made it into a fist and held it over his heart. Giving a half bow he said, "I promise."

And then he turned and silently slid open the door, disappearing into the pale mist with a great white hound trailing behind him.

@ @ @

The school year came to a close with little fanfare, the most exciting event being my deadly encounter with the dogs. By the end of my first week back, the most popular version of the story included some crude remark about starving coyotes and the only reason for my survival being that they weren't that desperate to eat someone like me.

But I didn't let it bother me. I was too fixated on missing Cade. As he had promised, Fergus stood watch at my back door every evening and even followed me to school. During lunch and the times in between classes, I would spot him on the edge of the woods, patiently watching me, making sure no nasty faelah were lurking about. It comforted me because even though Cade couldn't be there, I knew he still thought of me.

I still had trouble sleeping, though that was no big surprise. What with the emptiness I felt without Cade nearby combined with the memories of my ordeal. I never said anything to anyone about what I had learned about myself in the last several months, especially not my family. They had enough to worry about and I'm sure they would insist on taking me to another therapist if I started going into detail about the Faelorehn and my trip to the Otherworld. Nope, I'd had enough of therapists.

I would find a way to manage this on my own, even if it meant remaining vigilant around the clock because some horrifying fae beast could come jumping out at me at any moment. In my current state, I couldn't even outrun a snail, what with my cumbersome crutches. But nothing so much as a demented field mouse eyed me from the bushes in those final weeks before summer, and I was starting to think, no *dread*, that the Morrigan was gathering her troops to make one grand attack at some point in the future. Let's just say it didn't help with my insomnia.

Explanation

"So Stitch, what are your plans for summer?" Robyn said, breaking into my wandering thoughts.

I blanched at her new nickname for me. I knew she was trying to make light of the whole situation, and even though the stitches had come out a week ago, she still insisted on the moniker. I resorted to doing what I did best. I ignored the name.

"Hanging around the house probably. Maybe getting a job at one of the cafés in town, if they'll hire me."

It was truthful enough. I would be hanging around the house, hiding from Otherworldly monsters and waiting for Cade to come back. But I would also be preparing. I would take Fergus and go down into the swamp and practice my aim with the bow and special arrows Cade had given me, maybe even give my research into the world of the Celts a renewed visit. But for now, I'd enjoy the final days of being a junior in high school.

I sighed and looked around at my friends. We were all sprawled out on a patch of lawn by the track, taking advantage of the shade cast by a group of sycamores and eating our lunches. Thomas was trying to teach Will how to properly pronounce Spanish, Tully was finishing up some homework she had forgotten to do the night before, and Robyn was picking the black glitter nail polish off of her right index finger.

I smiled. How normal we all looked. But I knew the truth. I was far from being normal, I knew that for certain now, and although I was terrified of what the future might hold for a young Faelorehn in the mortal world, I would not be such a coward any more. I was no longer the timid Meghan Elam of Marshwood Lane in Arroyo Grande, but Meghan, Faelorehn of Eilé, and I would be ready for whatever that world had to throw at me.

Acknowledgments

A special thanks to all my professors in the Celtic Studies program at the University of California at Berkeley; for educating me in the mythos that has become the backbone of this series: may I not disappoint you with my creative twist of those sacred legends.

To my friends and family, who never stop supporting me in my crusade to create more worlds. Thank you for understanding that much of my free time belongs to this passion of mine.

Many thanks to P.A. Vannucci for designing the beautiful Faelorehn font for the Otherworld Trilogy.

Finally, a special thanks to Sr. Mary Keavey, for always believing in the things I could accomplish. Also, to Sr. Margaret Malone, who doesn't mind talking with me about the ancient Celtic tradition of her homeland.

About The Author

Jenna Elizabeth Johnson grew up and still resides on the Central Coast of California, the very location that has become the set of her novel, Faelorehn, and the inspiration for her other series, The Legend of Oescienne.

Miss Johnson has a degree in Art Practice with an emphasis in Celtic Studies from the University of California at Berkeley. She now draws much of her insight from the myths and legends of ancient Ireland to help set the theme for her books.

Besides writing and drawing, Miss Johnson enjoys reading, gardening, camping and hiking. In her free time (the time not dedicated to writing), she also practices the art of long sword combat and traditional archery.

For contact information, visit the author's website at:
www.jennaelizabethjohnson.com

Connect with Me Online:

Twitter: https://twitter.com/#!/jejoescienne

Facebook: https://www.facebook.com/pages/Jenna-Elizabeth-Johnson/202816013120106?sk=wall&filter=12

Other books by this author:

The Legend of Oescienne Series
The Finding (Book One)
The Beginning (Book Two)
The Awakening (Book Three)
Tales of Oescienne - A Short Story Collection

A sneak peek at the second book in the Otherworld Trilogy, Dolmarehn:

One

Absence

Fifty one days. Fifty one days ago Cade MacRoich walked out of my life like a ghost passing into the hereafter. And no, I haven't been obsessive enough to keep track of the hours and minutes, or even the seconds, but I've felt every last one of them. I probably wouldn't have been so fixated on his absence if he hadn't just up and left the way he did. Of course, at the time I was too distracted by my recent trauma to truly grasp what was going on.

Nearly a year ago I was under the impression that I was just a slightly abnormal teen. Sure, I'm tall and gangly and insecure like everybody else my age, but now I know just *how* different I am. Then one day this gorgeous guy shows up, out of nowhere, with a very simple explanation for all of my eccentricities: my changeable eyes, my tendency to hear voices and see things, the fact that I'd been found parentless as a toddler, roaming the streets of Los Angeles like a young girl who'd been separated from her mother in the women's clothing section of a super mall . . . He had come to tell me I was Faelorehn, immortal, from the Otherworld.

Shaking my head, I got back to work. Of course, watering Mrs. Dollard's plants didn't take much brain power. I had considered getting a part time job in town this past summer, but when the old lady had come over to ask if I could feed her cats and keep her yard alive while she was in Europe, I accepted right away. She was loaded and she always over-paid me. Besides, working in a café or at a local clothing store meant dealing with the public. I didn't do well with the public.

The sharp caw of a crow made me hit the ground like a soldier avoiding gunfire. If acting like an idiot wasn't bad enough, the hose got loose and soaked me. I glanced up and released a sigh of relief. Just a normal crow. I scrambled to my feet and tackled the hose before going over to shut it off. Yes, freaking out at the sound of a crow was weird for any normal person. But when you've spent the last several months dodging a Celtic goddess in raven form, well, any large black bird would give you the heebie-jeebies.

The garden was watered, Mrs. Dollard's five cats were sleeping off a food coma, and the afternoon sun was dipping low in the sky. The giant wet spot on my t-shirt was making me cold, and it was time I headed home anyways. Didn't want to get caught out after sunset. That's when the faelah are the most active . . .

A short bark greeted me as I made my way around the house. I smiled. A great white wolfhound with rusty colored ears sat patiently, panting and grinning.

"Hello Fergus. When's your master coming back?"

I placed a hand on his head and gave him a good scratch. He didn't answer my question, but I didn't expect him to.

Mrs. Dollard's was only a few houses down from my own. Before I stepped inside, however, I kept on walking to the end of the street, bypassing the *Dead End* sign. I had developed the habit of checking the knothole in the oak tree every day, hoping that Cade had left me a new note.

I frowned in disappointment when the knothole proved empty, but I wasn't surprised. Cade's absence was understandable. A few months ago, I had crossed into the Otherworld thinking that I was going to save him from some cruel fate. Turns out the Morrigan, one of the most powerful of all the Otherworldly deities, had merely wanted me where she could conveniently kill me. Still being pretty ignorant of my roots, I had believed her when she'd told me Cade needed my help. Hey, she'd been very convincing and well, I kind of had a huge crush on the guy, still do. And I'd say it's turned into something much more than a simple crush.

Pushing the hair out of my face, I climbed back up the slope and headed towards my bedroom on the basement floor of our house. I didn't like how much time I spent thinking about Cade; it couldn't be healthy, but he had saved my life after all. And he had been the one to tell me the truth about where I had come from.

My room greeted me with its usual chaos: various items of clothing spread about the floor and furniture, computer screen saver glowing blue and green, comforter and sheets wadded up into an unintelligible mess.

"Meghan!"

I jumped, and then grumbled. "What Logan?"

My younger brother, oldest of the five, stuck his head through the trap door that led up into the main part of the house. His blond hair fell to the side. I grinned. He looked like some miniature version of a pro surfer.

When his eyes found me he piped, "Dinner! Oh, and we're going to the beach for my birthday party tomorrow, remember?"

I cringed inwardly. Oh yeah. Forgot about that one. Logan had turned eleven just over a week ago, but he hadn't had his party because most of his friends were still on their summer vacations.

"Alright," I said, "be up in a minute."

Dolmarehn

Logan disappeared and I turned to look back through my sliding glass door. Fergus was gone, but I merely shrugged. He did that a lot. I wasn't sure if other people could see him or not (basically, I didn't know if he was visible to mortals), but maybe he didn't want to take the chance.

After quickly changing into a dry t-shirt and a pair of old sweat pants, I made my way up the spiral staircase and out into the circus that was the Elam family.

Mom was darting about the kitchen, getting the last minute dinner items ready, Dad was sitting in his recliner, as usual, reading the paper, and all five of my brothers, Logan, Bradley, Aiden and even the twins, Jack and Joey, were thoroughly engrossed in some science special on TV. I rolled my eyes. It was one of those 'deadliest insects' things and it included a detailed description of what they did that made them so dangerous. I felt my stomach churn when they started describing internal parasites.

"Boys, could you turn that off? We're about to eat dinner!"

Thank goodness for Mom.

We all sat down and tried to commence as a normal family would at mealtime. Too bad we weren't normal. One of us was a Faelorehn from the Otherworld. Of course, none of them knew about my true identity. Like the adoption agency that found me those many years ago, they thought I was just another abandoned human child. I knew if I told my mom and dad what I'd learned over the past year, they wouldn't be able to accept it. Or they would drag me off to another psychologist who would only prescribe mind-numbing medication. No thanks. I'd like to have all my wits about me when the Morrigan decided to attack again, thank you very much.

"Meg, you are coming with us tomorrow, correct?"

My dad's voice snapped me out of my train of thought. I grimaced. I really didn't want to go. Not that I had anything against Logan or birthday parties or even the beach, it's just that ever since my ordeal at the end of spring, I'd been very wary about wandering too far from home. That's what made Mrs. Dollard's offer so appealing. Only four houses down the road, I could manage that . . .

"Sure," I shrugged and stabbed at a few green beans.

"*Sure?*" Mom gave me one of her looks. "Meg, you've been practically cooped up in this house all summer. You only ever leave to take care of Matilda Dollard's cats, take those walks down into the swamp, or to visit Tully."

Okay, I had good reason not to wander far, reasons that had nothing to do with my fear of the faelah creatures creeping out of the dolmarehn hidden deep in the swamp. Up until a few weeks ago I had been in a leg cast, and that really limited my mobility. She couldn't really count visiting Tully, my best friend, as 'never going out'. Tully lived all the way at the head of our street. A good fifteen or so houses down. And my walks in the swamp were quite exciting, really. Or at least they had the potential to be. An Otherworldly creature could show up at any minute and cause quite a stir. And if that Otherworldly creature happened to be Cade . . .

I swallowed and put him as far out of my mind as possible. No need to get all dreamy-eyed at the dinner table. But really, my walks were productive. If Mom knew that I practiced with my longbow and arrows when I went down there, maybe she would change her mind. Of course, I only went down there alone because I knew Fergus would accompany me. If Cade's spirit guide wasn't around, I'd gladly admit defeat and take on the guise of a recluse.

"You have to go Meg!" Logan whined.

I glanced over at him, his blue eyes almost brimming with tears. I felt my heartstrings tighten. How could I deny my little brother anything?

I heaved a great sigh. "What beach again?"

Dolmarehn

"Avila," Dad said, "we're going to have a bonfire and everything, so be sure to bring your warm clothes. It'll get cold after dark."

I gritted my teeth despite my smile. *After dark* . . . I had been lucky the past few months. I'd only seen a handful of faelah wandering around in the swamp, but they had been small and Fergus had dealt with them. I had a feeling Fergus would not be accompanying me to the beach, and let's face it, it had just been too long since anything of great significance had happened. I was well over due for a good haunting.

Made in the USA
Charleston, SC
26 April 2015